"You're really ticked off, aren't you, that we tricked you into coming tonight?" Pierce said finally.

"Yes, really," Calico said.

"I don't blame you, I guess. It was a pretty juvenile plan, but desperate people do desperate things. You walked out of that café with every intention of walking out of my life as well. I just couldn't let that happen, Calico. Can't you see that?"

"Pierce, please—"

"I know you have things you want to accomplish. I promise I won't stand in your way. All I'm asking is that you make a little time for us."

"No. I can't, Pierce," Calico said quietly.

He moved in front of her, forcing her to stop walking. The star-studded sky cast a silvery glow over them. He framed her face in his hands, and she met his gaze with a frown.

"Believe me, Calico, it's people that matter, who they are inside, their values, that count. You have to give us a chance to find the answers to the questions we have about each other—"

"No, Pierce—"

"Questions, Calico Smith. Like what it would be like to kiss you"—he lowered his head toward hers—"in the moonlight, under the stars." He flicked his tongue over her lips and she shivered. "What you'd taste like, how soft your lips would be. Questions. So many questions."

He dropped his hands from her face, gathered her close to his body, and captured her mouth with his. . . .

WHAT ARE *LOVESWEPT* ROMANCES?

They are stories of true romance and touching emotion. We believe those two very important ingredients are constants in our highly sensual and very believable stories in the *LOVESWEPT* line. Our goal is to give you, the reader, stories of consistently high quality that may sometimes make you laugh, sometimes make you cry, but are always fresh and creative and contain many delightful surprises within their pages.

Most romance fans read an enormous number of books. Those they truly love, they keep. Others may be traded with friends and soon forgotten. We hope that each *LOVESWEPT* romance will be a treasure—a "keeper." We will always try to publish

LOVE STORIES YOU'LL NEVER FORGET
BY AUTHORS YOU'LL ALWAYS REMEMBER

The Editors

Loveswept 521

Joan Elliott Pickart
Irresistible

BANTAM BOOKS
NEW YORK • TORONTO • LONDON • SYDNEY • AUCKLAND

IRRESISTIBLE

A Bantam Book / January 1992

If you would be interested in receiving protective vinyl
covers for your Loveswept books, please write to this address
for information:

Loveswept
Bantam Books
P.O. Box 985
Hicksville, NY 11802

ISBN 0-553-44220-1

Published simultaneously in the United States and Canada

Bantam Books are published by Bantam Books, a division
of Bantam Doubleday Dell Publishing Group, Inc. Its trademark, consisting of the words "Bantam Books" and the
portrayal of a rooster, is Registered in U.S. Patent and
Trademark Office and in other countries. Marca Registrada.
Bantam Books, 666 Fifth Avenue, New York, New York
10103.

PRINTED IN THE UNITED STATES OF AMERICA

OPM   0 9 8 7 6 5 4 3 2 1

For Linda Snavely,
with a lot of thanks,
for a lot of things.

One

Pierce Anderson pulled the faded flannel robe more tightly over his pajama-covered chest and took the thermometer from his mouth. He peered at the glass tube, then groaned as he placed it on the end table next to the big leather chair he was sprawled in.

Oh, he was sick, he thought gloomily. So, so sick. He was have-to-die-to-get-better sick. A fever of a hundred and one was serious, by damn, and he ached from head to toe. Even his hair hurt, and his eyelashes, and his teeth.

He turned his head to study the myriad bottles containing a wide variety of medications, which were lined up on the table like soldiers at the ready. A stack of freshly laundered and folded pristine white handkerchiefs was within reach. He lifted his watch from the yellow legal pad of paper next to the handkerchiefs, then picked up the pad.

After checking the time and carefully scrutinizing the information on the top sheet of paper, he nodded and snapped free the pen he'd clipped to the pad. He made an entry on the ever-growing list, then returned paper and pen to the table. His hand hovered over the bottles until he found what he was seeking. Moments later he swallowed two pills, which had been dutifully recorded on the paper, draining the last of the orange juice from his glass.

Sighing a rather sad and weary sigh, he leaned his head back and closed his eyes.

He was so sick, he mused, as he began to drift off to sleep. Well, at least he had his personal affairs in order. His will was prepared, beneficiaries were named on the proper document on file with his stockbroker. If the Grim Reaper came and tapped him on the shoulder, saying he was about to be reaped, at least he'd die organized.

His poor mother, he thought foggily. She'd be distraught. She might even skip a bridge game or two. No, probably not. She'd wear black to a few bridge sessions, though, out of respect for his untimely demise. That was better than nothing.

And his sister? She'd stop changing diapers long enough to have a good, loud cry about her dearly departed little brother. No, she'd probably have to cry *while* she was changing diapers, considering the fact that she had six-month-old triplets. Well, that was a more comforting scenario than her not finding time to cry at all.

Pierce yawned, then slouched lower in the chair, his eyes still closed.

He hoped there wouldn't be too many flowers at his funeral. He'd had a terrible reaction to flowers ever since he'd been struck down in his prime by allergies two weeks after his twenty-first birthday. Surely his mother or sister would remember, despite their grief, to tell people . . . not . . . to send . . . flowers. . . .

Pierce Anderson slept.

A little over an hour later, a steady thudding noise caused Pierce to stir and slowly open his eyes. He stared blankly into space, vaguely aware that the noise matched the throbbing cadence of the ache in his head. He blinked, blinked again, then realized that the rhythmic thud was coming from the apartment door.

Great, he thought. He was a dying man, and some jerk was standing outside his door waiting to sell him encyclopedias. What he needed was a cemetery plot. Well, forget it, he wasn't moving his germ-ridden body to go answer the damn door.

But the steady knocking went on, and on, and on.

Muttering an expletive that would have brought a cluck of disapproval from his bridge-playing mother, Pierce pushed himself to his feet. He waited for a wave of dizziness to pass, then shuffled across the room, his feet half in, half out, of his sloppy corduroy slippers.

He opened the door, took one look at what was standing in the corridor, then slammed the door closed so hard, the medicine bottles on the table clinked and clattered.

"Ohmigod," he said.

Whirling around, he flattened himself against the door, arms spread out to further enforce the barricade between himself and that . . .

"Oh, Lord. Oh, help," he said, pressing one hand to his forehead.

He was burning up with fever, he thought frantically. He didn't feel that hot, but what other explanation could there be? He was hallucinating because his brain was fried. What he'd imagined he'd seen in the hallway really hadn't been there.

There was not a human-size chicken beyond that door!

The knocking began again. Pierce jerked away from the door and spun around to stare at it, then groaned as the motion intensified the pain in his head.

"Hello? Hello?" a muffled voice called from behind the door.

Pierce slapped his hand back onto his forehead and left it there.

That's nice, he thought, ready to give in to panic. The human-size chicken that wasn't really there could talk. Fascinating. It was in Technicolor, too, with bright yellow feathers and a neon-orange beak. It was a little under six feet tall, and wasn't a bad-looking chicken, as far as life-size, imaginary chickens went.

"Hello?" the chicken called. "I'm sorry to disturb you, but I really need your help. Sir?"

A chicken in need, Pierce mused wearily, was a chicken, indeed.

With that profound thought, one hand still clamped over his throbbing forehead, he opened the door, swept his arm through the air in a gesture of welcome, and watched the imaginary, life-size chicken waddle into his living room.

"Nice tail," he said, closing the door. "The three big red feathers on your tush are a classy touch."

"Oh, you're ill," the chicken said. Its voice was still muffled, even though the door was no longer between them. "I apologize for bothering you, but no one else seems to be home. Headache?"

"Body ache," he said. "You have the right apartment, anyway. I'm the one who conjured you up in my fever-racked brain."

"Pardon me?"

"You know, you're a fever-induced illusion. I wonder what conclusion a psychologist would draw from the fact that my mind produced a chicken? There must be some deep-seated message here. Are you a girl chicken? Your voice isn't clear, but you do sound like a girl. Well, sure, or else you'd be a rooster. Right?"

"Huh?" The chicken's gaze swept over the multitude of bottles on the table. "What are you taking? You're not making an awful lot of sense, you know what I mean?"

"I'm a sick man," he said indignantly.

"No joke," the chicken said. "I won't argue with you on that point. If you could help me for about two seconds, I'll be on my way."

"Oh, sure thing," he said, finally dropping his hand from his forehead. "Let it not be said that Pierce Anderson stood idly by and didn't assist a chicken with a dilemma. My mother would be banned from the bridge brigade of Stuart, Florida. Personally, I like living here in Phoenix, but my mom had her heart set on retiring to Florida, so off she went about four years ago. Well, you know all this, because you're a product of my mind."

"Whatever you say, Pierce Anderson," the chicken said quickly.

"What is it you need help with?"

"Oh, well, you see, I guess I caught the edge of my head in the zipper on my body, and I'm stuck."

He stared into space. "Maybe I should take my temperature again."

"Look, Pierce . . . I'll call you Pierce, okay?" The chicken turned her back to him. "There, at the end of my head right at the neck. Is the material jammed in the zipper?"

Pierce leaned over and peered at the subject matter, brushing a bunch of feathers aside and narrowing his eyes.

"Yep," he said, nodding, "your head is caught in the zipper to your body, all right." He suddenly straightened, his eyes wide. "You're wearing a chicken suit. That means you're not really a chicken."

"Well, gosh and golly," the chicken said dryly, "what a news flash. I may, however, remain a chicken for the rest of my life if you don't help me out of this thing."

"What in the hell are you doing walking around in a chicken suit in the middle of the afternoon? Do you have any idea what it does to a sick man's mind?"

"Believe me, you've made it clear what's going on in your sick mind. Would you please quit yelling and unstick my zipper?"

"Oh. Well, sure. Let me see what I can do here."

For the next few minutes, Pierce concentrated on his mission. He tugged at the material, wiggled the zipper tab, tugged and wiggled, wiggled and tugged, until . . .

"Victory!" he shouted.

The chicken jumped at his sudden, loud outburst.

"Now what?" he asked. "Should I unzip the whole thing? I mean, are you decent under your feathers?"

"Oh, for Pete's sake. A person doesn't go around stark naked when they're being a chicken."

"Well, excuse me, but I'm not up on the current social etiquette for chickendom. Okay, here I go."

As Pierce slid the long zipper down, the chicken reached up, lifted off the head, and dropped it onto the floor. The body of feathers fell from her shoulders to pool at her feet. She stepped free of the yellow pile, turning at once to smile her thanks.

And Pierce Anderson stopped breathing.

Oh, Lord, he thought, finally remembering to take a breath, if this was a fever-induced illusion, he was staying sick for the rest of his life. No, she was real. Oh, was she ever real. She was small boned and stood about five feet four, and had short curly black hair. Her features were delicate, and she possessed a natural beauty, a fresh-air-and-sunshine prettiness that needed no makeup.

And her eyes. They were the biggest, bluest eyes he'd ever seen. And her smile was the warmest, the sweetest . . . He dragged his gaze from her face. She wore a red T-shirt, its worn, faded fabric softly clinging to her small breasts, and white shorts revealed a long length of legs that looked soft and satiny, alluring and sexy . . . She was the most fantastic undressed chicken imaginable.

"Thank you so much, Pierce Anderson," she said, extending her hand. "I'm Calico Smith."

He took her hand in his. "Charmed."

Tingles of warmth raced up Calico's arm at the feel of his strong hand closing around hers. Pierce Anderson, she mused, was scrumptious. If this was how he looked sick as a dog, he had to be drop-dead gorgeous when fit as a fiddle.

He was, she guessed, about six feet tall. His shoulders were wide, and despite the old bathrobe he wore, she was positive there wasn't an ounce of unwanted fat on his trim body.

His face was composed of hard lines and sharp angles—undeniably handsome and indubitably masculine—yet his lips appeared soft, tender . . . sensual. His hair was dark and thick and conservatively cut, and his brown eyes were surrounded by the longest lashes she'd ever seen on a man.

He'd looked delicious when she'd been peering at him through a bunch of feathers that had kept flopping in front of her eyes. But now? Holy Toledo.

"There are women," she said, her gaze riveted on his face, "who would kill to have eyelashes like yours."

"Oh, please." He rolled his eyes. "I've been hearing about my eyelashes for nearly thirty years. I'd trade them in for a shorter set if I could." He paused, frowning. "I think it's time for my antihistamines."

"Well, you'd better get to it, then. May I have my hand back, please?"

"What?" Pierce looked down at their still-linked hands. "Oh, I didn't realize I was . . ." He released her hand with a reluctance that surprised him, then decided it was simply because he'd had no human contact for three days. "I'd better sit down. I'm very sick, you know." He sprawled into the big leather chair. "Oh, my aching self."

"Do you have the flu?"

"Bubonic plague," he said, closing his eyes.

She laughed. "Oh, for heaven's sake."

He opened one eye. "It's not funny." Also not

funny, he thought, was the bolt of heat that had rocketed through his exhausted body at the sound of Calico's laughter. Calico. It certainly was an unusual name, but for some reason, it fit her. "Why are you a chicken?" He closed his eye.

"I was passing out samples of a new frozen chicken dinner in a supermarket. They set up a microwave oven, you see, and I zap the stuff, then hand it out in bite-size pieces on colored toothpicks. Part of the deal is to come to the store and leave in my chicken outfit so I can push the product on the bus."

"Oh."

"It's amazing. Not one person on the bus asks me why I'm a chicken. Can you beat that? You'd think chickens rode buses in Phoenix every day of the week. When I got home today, I discovered my head was caught in my body, and here I am. I'm apartment-sitting next door. Your neighbor went on a cruise, and I moved in there yesterday. I water the plants, bring in the mail, feed the goldfish, whatever."

"Oh."

"Poor little fish. What a boring life. He just swims back and forth in his glass bowl. At least he has colored marbles on the bottom to look at." She glanced around. "I like what you've done to your apartment. Earth tones are nice. The lady next door is into flowers. Every piece of furniture is upholstered in a fabric with a different flower." She laughed. "I hope I don't get carried away and water the sofa. This certainly is a classy neighborhood, and these apartments are huge. Are you married?"

Pierce's eyes popped open. "Where did that come from? I'm still back at bored goldfish and flowered sofas."

"Well, this is a big place for one person. So, it's reasonable for me to ask whether or not you're married. I'd hate for your wife to get all in a tizzy because you unzipped a chicken."

He laughed, but in the next instant he frowned, pressing the heels of his hands to his temples.

"Don't do that," he said, moaning. "If you make me laugh, my head will fall right off." He dropped his hands. "No, I'm not married. I've never been married. The way I feel, I won't live long enough to even find the woman I want to marry."

"Really, Pierce, I somehow doubt you're going to croak from a simple case of the flu."

"One never knows. As for this apartment, it meets my needs. I bring a lot of work home with me, and I've turned one bedroom into an office of sorts. I'm an architect. Anderson Architects, Incorporated. Have you ever heard of it?"

"No, I can't say that I have. Of course, I haven't had a house built for myself in ages." She laughed again. "What a bizarre thought. I don't own a car, let alone a house. Is there anything I can get for you before I go? I can't imagine what it would be, because you have enough medication here to open a drugstore."

"Would you mind filling my glass with orange juice? There's a pitcher in the refrigerator."

She picked up the empty glass from the end

table. "I'll be back in a flash. I assume your kitchen is in the same place as Mrs. Weatherby's next door."

He nodded cautiously, then turned his aching head to watch her cross the room.

Very, *very* nice, he thought, enjoying her light, almost bouncy stride, the slight sway of her sweetly rounded hips. She certainly was lovely, in a homespun, refreshing way, but she wasn't his type. He dated career women, older women, more mature and experienced. Calico appeared to be only twenty-two or twenty-three. And the women he knew wouldn't be caught dead masquerading as a chicken.

They also, he admitted, wouldn't come within a hundred yards of him while he was sick. They might catch his dread disease and miss a few days of work. He couldn't think of one woman who would hang around his germ-laden living room and bring him a glass of orange juice.

Was that depressing? he wondered, then told himself to forget it. His head hurt too much to concentrate on anything.

"Here you go," Calico said cheerfully, coming back into the room. She put the glass on the end table, then scooped up the chicken outfit from the floor. "Thanks again, Pierce. Don't move, I can let myself out. I hope you feel better real soon."

"I probably will, but then again . . ."

"Chin up, old dear," she said breezily. " 'Bye for now."

The door closed behind her as she left the apartment, and a heavy silence fell.

"Good-bye, Calico," Pierce said to the empty room.

A yellow feather had dropped from her chicken suit and lay on the floor by his chair. With one hand pressed to his forehead, he leaned over and picked it up. He stared at it, and was astonished to realize he was smiling. He sobered almost immediately.

"Antihistamines," he mumbled. "I'm overdue for my antihistamines. Damn, I screwed up the schedule."

An hour later, Calico leaned her head back against the marble wall surrounding the bathtub and sighed with sheer pleasure. As she relaxed in the warm water, she inhaled the delicate aroma of the mounds of lilac-scented bubbles.

She should be studying, she knew, but she'd give herself ten more minutes in this wonderfully soothing bath. This was the epitome of luxury, and Mrs. Weatherby had generously told Calico to feel free to use any of the many bath products that were displayed on the large marble vanity. There were more jars, bottles, and tubes of lotions and creams and cleansers than Pierce Anderson had in his drugstore collection of medication.

Pierce Anderson, she mused, sinking lower in the fragrant water, with the scrumptious body, astonishingly handsome face, and killer eye-lashes. Goodness gracious, those eyelashes were really something. If he died of the flu, which he seemed to think was a definite possibility, he should will his eyelashes to science.

Despite his ancient bathrobe and shabby slippers, he was obviously a man with money. No doubt he designed million-dollar homes for people and got paid enormous commissions. He lived alone in his grand apartment—and she didn't even want to think how much it cost—because it met his needs and he could afford it. It was as simple as that, and it was how people like Pierce were used to living. Want it? Buy it.

She pressed a toe against the lever that would open the drain and whisk away her delicious bubble bath. Reluctantly she left the tub and dried herself off with one of the biggest, fluffiest towels she'd ever seen.

Someday, she thought, as she donned fresh underwear, then a baggy pink sweatshirt and faded jeans. Someday she'd have a nice place to live, pretty clothes to wear, cupboards that nearly overflowed with food.

Well, she thought, smiling as she flicked a brush through her hair, she wouldn't live on the same scale as Pierce Anderson and Mrs. Weatherby. Not even close. But that was fine, because what would a woman with her background have in common with people who flitted off to the Caribbean for a vacation and who didn't think twice of eating out at expensive restaurants four nights a week? She'd be perfectly content with a cozy little place to live and enough groceries on hand to assure her of her next few meals. Oh, yes, someday, someday.

She left the bathroom and headed for the kitchen, which contained so many gadgets, she'd decided she'd exhaust her brain if she attempted to figure out what they all were used for.

She had a supper consisting of a grilled cheese sandwich and a mug of tomato soup, fed the goldfish—poor bored thing—then curled up in the corner of the marshmallow-soft velvet sofa. Opening a large textbook, she found the page she was looking for, then stared into space for a long moment.

"Why, Pierce Anderson," she said aloud to no one, batting her eyelashes. "How divine to see you again after all these years. Are you still designing marvelous houses, or buildings, or whatever it is you design? . . . Me? Oh, haven't you heard? I have my own business. I'm a certified public accountant, darling, and clients are flocking to my door. I've got to dash, but we must do lunch."

She frowned.

"Calico Smith, shut up and study," she said.

Ridiculous daydreams, she admonished herself. Oh, she was determined to be a CPA, but she would never belong to the world that Pierce inhabited with, she didn't doubt, great ease. She'd accepted facts like that one long ago.

She could remember stopping and gazing at the huge houses with their manicured lawns as she'd walked home from school. But then she'd go farther, to where she belonged, in the shabby but sparkling clean apartment she shared with Gran. The lessons she'd learned then held true now. Chickens who rode buses didn't hobnob with the wealthy.

Calico forced her attention back to her book, but before she began reading she thought, Pierce Anderson really did have the most gorgeous eyelashes she'd ever seen.

Two

Pierce spent a fitful night, tossing and turning whenever he was halfway between being awake and asleep, and having disturbing dreams whenever he dozed.

The last dream he had as dawn crept over the horizon and chased away the darkness of night, was an exhausting scenario in which he was being followed by a giant chicken through a maze constructed of orange juice cans.

The feathered fowl kept hollering at him to stop, as he continually lost his way in the maze. Why he felt he had to escape from the chicken, he didn't know, but his efforts were useless. Every path led to one dead end after another.

At seven o'clock he finally gave up on sleep and staggered into his bathroom. He showered and shaved, then stared at his reflection in the mirror.

Gray, he decided. He definitely looked gray.

And old. No one would argue with him if he said he was pushing forty, instead of thirty. He'd aged overnight, and wouldn't be a bit surprised if his hair started to fall out. He was a physical wreck, brought down by a flu, and except for Calico getting him a fresh glass of orange juice, he'd received no sympathy or tender loving care.

Sighing another of his sad and weary sighs, he left the bathroom. In his bedroom he dressed in a gray suit—to match the pallor of his face—a pale blue shirt, and a dark gray tie.

As he waited for his coffee to brew, he checked his pulse rate, took his temperature, and frowned when the thermometer declared that he was normal.

He didn't feel normal, he thought glumly. He felt rotten, weak, achy, and he was none too pleased with Calico Smith for chasing him through the orange-juice-can maze during the seemingly endless night.

After pouring himself a mug of steaming coffee, he sank onto a chair at the table. That *had* been Calico in the chicken suit in his dream, he reasoned. Who else could it have been? She was the only human-size chicken he knew.

Cheerful and cute Calico.

Cute? he pondered, sipping the hot coffee. The description fit, he supposed, because she wasn't stunningly gorgeous. But when she'd first emerged from her feathers the day before, he'd been struck by her aura of fresh air and sunshine. No, cute didn't fully describe the uniqueness of Calico.

Why was he wearing out his already depleted brain thinking about her? he wondered. Of course, it was understandable, considering the fact that she'd chased him around a maze instead of allowing him to get the proper rest he needed. Calico was *not* a considerate chicken.

And he, Pierce decided, was beginning to sound like a total idiot. He had to get to the office. Since he'd been away, *dying* of the flu, for three days, he could just imagine the paperwork his secretary Miriam had piled on his desk.

He'd told Miriam not to disturb him at home while he was dying, but since she looked like a grandmother and had known him most of his life, he'd thought she would have at least telephoned to see if he was still breathing.

Shaking his head, Pierce rose, set his empty mug in the sink, and left his apartment, briefcase in hand. He walked down the carpeted corridor and stepped into the elevator.

"Wait!" a voice called. "Hold the elevator, please."

He pressed the button to keep the doors open, and a moment later, Calico Smith ran into the elevator, teetering to a stop beside him.

"Thanks a million," she said, smiling up at him. "How are you feeling this morning, Pierce?"

"Terrible," he said. "Going down?"

"What? Oh, yes, down." She hefted the strap of her canvas tote bag higher onto her shoulder.

For someone who felt terrible, she mused,

Pierce Anderson certainly looked good. Great, even. Dreamboat wonderful. And, she thought, surveying his well-tailored suit and classy leather briefcase, if an alien landed from outer space, Pierce could be used as an example of the classic "upwardly mobile young person." He even had his initials in gold lettering on his briefcase.

Despite her knowing that she and Pierce Anderson had nothing in common, Calico's heart was beating like a bongo drum. Since she was in excellent physical condition, she couldn't chalk it up to her mad dash down the hall. No, it was Pierce, who looked sensational—albeit a tad pale—and smelled like soap and musky after-shave, who was causing her heart to go nuts, while her stomach did a funny little flutter dance. This would never do.

"You're not a chicken today," Pierce said.

She was a woman, he added silently. In jeans and a green T-shirt, her dark curls shining and blue eyes sparkling. She was definitely not a chicken.

She laughed. "I'll be a chicken later this afternoon. I have classes this morning."

The elevator bumped gently to a stop, and the doors slid open on the ground floor.

" 'Bye," she said.

"Hey, wait a minute." He followed her out of the elevator. "Classes?"

"At ASU, ol' Arizona State University. I really can't chat now, Pierce, or I'll miss my bus."

"Well, Calico, I—I could drop you off on campus."

"Oh, I wouldn't want you to go out of your way."

"No problem. I have an errand to tend to near there before I go to my office."

"Are you sure?"

"Sure, I'm sure. Come on. My car is in the underground garage." And he was full of bull, he thought. He didn't have an errand in Tempe near the campus. His office was there in Scottsdale, many miles in the opposite direction from ASU. He *knew* that fever had fried his brain. "Let's go."

They stepped back onto the elevator, and Pierce pressed a button. Moments later the elevator doors opened again to reveal the cavernous, brightly lit garage. He immediately whipped a clean handkerchief from his back pants pocket and held it against his nose and mouth.

Calico glanced up at him, then did a quick double take. "Are you going to sneeze?"

He shook his head. "Lingering exhaust fumes," he said, his voice muffled. "People have finally become aware of the danger to their health from secondhand smoke from cigarettes, cigars, and pipes. But what about exhaust fumes? This garage is a disease waiting to happen. I'm talking about respiratory illnesses, lung and heart trouble, allergies, asthma, gastrointestinal problems. . . . You just wouldn't believe how long the list is."

She looked around as though searching for the culprits he had named.

"Gastrointestinal problems?" she repeated.

"Absolutely," he said. "My car is that blue one right ahead there."

She recognized the sleek lines of a Mazda Miata.

"A sports car? They have big, powerful engines." And, she added silently, big, powerful price tags. That car definitely cost more than the total amount of money that had passed through her hands during her lifetime. She cast him a wry look, unwilling to acknowledge the defensiveness that made her ask, "Aren't you adding an awful lot of exhaust fumes to the ozone layer, or whatever?"

Pierce slipped the handkerchief back into his pocket, then unlocked and opened the passenger door. As she started to get into the car, he helped her in a gentlemanly fashion, lightly holding her arm. Yet even that light and almost impersonal touch sent sparks zinging through her, more potent than what she'd felt the day before when he held her hand. She made a big show of settling her heavy tote bag at her feet to cover her sudden sensual awareness of him, and almost sighed with relief when he shut the door.

Then she stiffened when he opened the driver's door and slid behind the wheel, and she realized just how very small his spiffy sports car was. She stared straight ahead, determined not to let him get to her.

"You're right about exhaust fumes," he said as he started the engine with a muted roar, "but I cut down on polluted exhaust by keeping my vehicle in top condition." He drove up the ramp of the garage and merged with the heavy morning rush-hour traffic. "If more people maintained their automobiles in a proper manner, thus reducing fumes, there would be an increase in productivity in the workplace as fewer employees would be ill. And buses. They are big pollution offenders. You really shouldn't ride on buses, Calico."

She smiled at him, a little bemusedly. "You're really into this stuff, aren't you? As for buses, I have to get where I'm going, you know."

"You should consider wearing a surgical mask when you're riding on a bus then."

Calico swallowed a burst of laughter. "I'll give it some thought." Time to change the subject, she mused. "I hope it doesn't get too hot today. That chicken suit is grim, because it gets awfully warm in there. We've had fairly cool weather for early May."

"Most things are in bloom, though. It's a bad time for allergies. I have terrible allergies."

Oh, my, Calico thought, smiling again. Pierce Anderson was a tad on the neurotic side regarding germs, diseases, and such. She should be rolling her eyes and thinking how sad it was that someone so gorgeous could be so paranoid. Instead, she was finding his overreactions rather endearing.

"What are you studying at ASU?" he asked, stopping at a red light.

"Accounting. I graduate at the end of this month with a bachelor's degree. Then I take the test in June to qualify to be a CPA. The mere thought of that test gives me cold chills. I'll pass it, though. I have to."

The light turned green, and Pierce sped away from the intersection.

"You sound very determined," he said.

"I am. I'm twenty-three years old. It's taken me forever, it seems, to get this far, because I've had to work part-time the whole way through college. And you should see the student loans I have to pay back. Being a CPA instead of just an accountant will open doors for me to much better jobs. I am going to pass that test."

Pierce glanced at her, intrigued by the intensity he heard in her voice. How long had it been, he mused, since he'd felt as passionate about something, as Calico was about becoming a CPA? Had he *ever* been that driven, that determined? Not that he could recall. Everything had been so easy. He'd always had plenty of money at his disposal, and when he'd settled on his career choice, he'd gone out and done it.

As soon as he'd gotten his degree, he'd started his own business, and that had been that. The first year had been lean as far as clients went, but he'd had financial resources to see him through. Now he was considered one of the finest young architects in the valley.

Why, he wondered, did the overview of his life

suddenly seem bleak and empty, as though something of major importance was missing? Oh, forget it, he told himself. His mind, as well as his body, was still limp from his horrendous bout of the flu. He probably should have spent another day at home resting but—he sighed silently—a man had to do what a man had to do. That was life.

But why, he pondered, did he feel a ridiculous urge to apologize to Calico, just because he'd never had to be a chicken?

Calico waved as Pierce pulled away from the curb. He answered with a toot of the horn, then eased his sleek car into the traffic and quickly disappeared. She stood still for a long moment, then started down the sidewalk.

"Hey, Calico," a voice called, "wait up."

She stopped and turned, smiling as she watched a tall—very tall—man dressed in jeans and a faded ASU T-shirt loping toward her. He was good-looking in a boyish way, and his head was covered by a mass of tight blond curls. He covered the distance in short order, and halted his flight when he reached her. She tilted her head back, way back, to meet his gaze.

"Hi, Sticks," she said.

"Hello, love of my life," he said.

They set off down the sidewalk, Sticks shortening his stride as much as possible so that Calico could keep up.

"Okay, confess," he said. "Where'd you snag Mr. Megabucks?"

"Pardon me?"

"The car, Calico. I saw the mean machine. What a vehicle. When I make the pros in basketball, I'm going to get something like that."

"I don't think you could fold up enough to drive one of those."

"No? Well, damn." He shrugged. "I'll have it custom-made to accommodate my gorgeous long legs."

"Good idea."

"So? Who was he?"

"Oh, he's my temporary neighbor. His name is Pierce Anderson, and he's an architect. I met him yesterday when my head got stuck in my body."

Sticks frowned for a moment, then nodded. "While you were a chicken, right?"

"Yep."

"As the big brother figure in your life, Calico, it's my responsibility to warn you about rich playboy types who drive fancy cars."

"Okay," she said, laughing, "I'll consider myself warned."

"I mean it. You're apartment-sitting out there in Scottsdale, which is filled with people who are filthy rich. He's not your type, that flashy architect."

"For Pete's sake, you don't even know him."

"Add up the data, babycakes. He's not for you."

"Well, darn," she said. "I guess I'll have to call off the wedding then."

"Would you get serious?"

"You're the one talking nonsense, Sticks. I just met Pierce Anderson yesterday." And nearly fainted dead at his feet. "He's a nice person. Period." With a fantastic physique and the most incredible eyelashes she'd ever seen. "He offered me a ride this morning because he had to come this way. End of story." Except for little details like how beautiful Pierce looked in his banker's suit, how good he smelled, and how she'd been strangely weak in the knees when she'd gotten out of his car. "I named Mrs. Weatherby's goldfish Homer. Even a goldfish deserves a name, don't you think?"

"What I think," Sticks said, "is that it's very scary that I understand everything you say. There was a time when I couldn't keep up, you know. Now you make sense, and that's frightening."

"You're crazy."

"That, my sweet petunia, is the point I'm trying to make."

"Oh, hush. I propped open a magazine by Homer's bowl this morning. It shows a picture of snow-covered mountains in Colorado. I thought it would be a nice change from colored marbles."

"You'll probably mess up the little guy's psyche."

"Oh, dear, I hope not."

"Gotta leave you, sweets," Sticks said, halting

in front of a building. "Are we still on for to-night? You're going to help me with my calculus, aren't you?"

"Sure. You have the address, don't you?"

"Glued to my brain. I'm borrowing Hoop Henderson's car. Well, he calls it a car. I guess it's a car because it has tires, a steering wheel, and an engine. But I swear, it looks like a junkyard that moves."

"It'll get you where you need to go. I'll see you tonight."

"'Bye, my pretty magnolia." He sprinted off across the grass.

Calico smiled as she watched him go, then her smile faded and was replaced by a frown.

Sticks was a good friend, she mused. They'd spent a lot of time together in the three years she'd known him. He had one more year at ASU, then hopefully he'd be signing with a professional basketball team.

A lot of people, Calico knew, believed that she and Sticks were an item. That was fine with her. She didn't have time for the dating scene, so didn't correct anyone who mentioned her "boy-friend" Sticks Statler.

Of course, her friend Abby, who rented a room in the same run-down house as Calico, knew that Calico and Sticks were like brother and sister. Abby was head over heels in love with Sticks, but the big basketball player hadn't figured that out yet.

Calico sighed. Life was very complicated. Abby loved Sticks, Sticks loved basketball, people thought Sticks loved Calico, and Calico loved . . . no one. And Pierce Anderson? she wondered. Who would he fall in love with? Oh, for heaven's sake, where had that thought come from?

She glanced at her watch, then quickened her step, determined not to be late for class.

Pierce strode down the carpeted corridor to the reception area of Anderson Architects, Incorporated. The woman seated behind the desk there was engaged in a telephone conversation, and he frowned in annoyance.

As she continued talking with a client, he restlessly paced the plushly furnished room, glaring repeatedly at the woman. She met his glowering looks one for one.

"Miriam," he finally mouthed, "hang up."

The plump gray-haired woman wrinkled her nose at him. He threw up his hands and resumed his trek back and forth in front of her.

"That does it," Miriam said at last to the client. "Our schedule is coordinated with yours. The plans will be in your hands by next Tuesday with the changes you've requested. I'll give these notes to Michael the minute he comes in, and if he has any questions he'll give you a call . . . Thank you, Mrs. Howlett. It was lovely speaking with you . . . Yes, you have a nice day too . . . Good-bye for now."

She replaced the receiver, and Pierce instantly halted in front of her desk.

"Miriam—"

"Pierce Anderson," she interrupted, "you're driving me straight up the wall. If you ask me once more what the temperature is outside, I'm going to scream. You have a fancy stereo and tape deck gizmo in your office, and you have an ear sticking out of each side of your head so that you can hear. News briefs and weather are broadcast every hour."

"You put a call through to me, Miriam," Pierce exclaimed, "and I missed the four o'clock report. Phone the weather bureau and ask how hot it is."

Miriam folded her arms over her ample breasts. "No. They recognize my voice now. It's ridiculous and embarrassing, and I refuse to call them again, especially when I have no idea why I'm doing it."

Pierce grimaced. The reason why he didn't call the weather bureau himself was because they recognized his voice too. He planted his hands flat on Miriam's desk and leaned toward her. "I want you to call because it's hotter today than yesterday. I'm concerned about heatstroke, dehydration, dizzy spells."

"You're in a temperature-controlled office complex, Pierce. There is nothing wrong with you except for being a little pale from having had the flu. Trust me, dear, you're fine."

"I am *not* fine, Miriam," he said, his jaw clenching. "I am in a weakened physical state due to having had a vicious case of the flu. Not that you bothered to check up on me to see if I'd died during my illness."

"You told me not to disturb you."

"That's beside the point. You could have at least—No, forget my flu. Not that you ever did give it much thought. I need to know the temperature outside. Miriam, this is serious. If you were a human-size chicken and had to ride the bus after passing out colored toothpicks, you'd realize that the weather could have a tremendous effect on your physical well-being."

Miriam's eyes widened and her mouth dropped open as she stared at Pierce. She shook her head slightly, then snapped her mouth closed.

"Oh, mercy," she murmured, her shocked gaze riveted on Pierce. "Your fussing and worrying about every tiny threat to your health has finally pushed you over the edge of sanity. I should have known this would happen. You took it so personally when you suddenly became susceptible to allergies nine years ago. My darling boy, listen to me. You've got to seek help, talk to a psychologist, before it's too late." She paused. "A human-size chicken? Oh, bless your poor mother's heart. Her only son is a fruit-cake."

Pierce smacked the desk with the palm of one hand. "Dammit, Miriam . . . Ow, that hurt." He straightened and scrutinized his stinging hand. "I'll probably get tendinitis," he muttered.

Miriam pulled the telephone book from a

drawer, thudded it onto her desk, and began to flip through the pages with a frenzy.

"What you're going to get," she said, "is the finest care available. You can afford the best, and we won't rest until your mentally unbalanced condition is un-unbalanced, or rebalanced, or however they describe fixing up someone whose brain has all the characteristics of scrambled eggs." She sniffled. "You dear thing, this is so incredibly sad."

"That's it!" Pierce shouted. "You're fired."

"Hush. I'm trying to read the fine print here. Goodness, these shrinks are certainly specialized. If you're completely bonkers, you'd probably have to see fifteen different doctors."

"Miriam!"

She jumped in her chair and stared at him again.

"I am not insane," he said tightly, "despite the fact that I have to deal with you every day. As for the human-size chicken—"

"Who rides the bus," Miriam interjected, "with colored toothpicks."

"No, she rides the bus after *passing out* the colored toothpicks."

"Sorry. I'll try to keep the details straight." She sniffled again. "I'll stand by you through all of this, Pierce. You won't be alone, dear."

"Oh, good Lord," he said, dragging his hands through his hair. Staring up at the ceiling, he took a deep breath, let it out slowly, then looked at Miriam again. "The chicken is a person, a woman, who wears a chicken suit that has a tricky zipper that causes her head to get caught in her body. She has to ride the bus as part of the job of passing out food samples in a grocery store. The chicken's name is Calico Smith. The stupid suit is hot; hence, my concern about the temperature. Are you following me here, Miriam?"

"Oh," she said, nodding slowly. "All this concern about the weather is because of a woman?" A bright smile lit up her face. "Well, imagine that. A woman. You have your share of women, of course, but I've never known you to get in a dither like this over one of them. Calico Smith. Well, my stars, isn't this interesting?" She propped her elbows on the desk, laced her fingers beneath her chin, and smiled up at him. "Tell me all about Calico Smith. Don't leave out anything."

Pierce narrowed his eyes. "No."

"Why not? Haven't I proven over the years that I love you like a son? Haven't I been a mother figure to you since your own went off to soak up the rays and play bridge twenty-four hours a day? Don't I keep the cabinet here filled with all the medications that you require be on hand at all times, including one dozen—not eleven, not thirteen—but one dozen boxes of tissues at the ready?"

He nodded. "All of the above is true."

"So? Fill me in on Calico Smith. What a darling name."

"Miriam," Pierce said, crossing his arms over his chest, "I'm not going to tell you one blasted thing. Why? Item one." He held up a finger. "You and my bridge-playing mother are very close friends. You talk on the phone every Sunday night at seven, and gossip so fast and furious, it's a wonder you don't need oxygen. Item two." Up popped another finger. "Calico is a woman, yes, and a chicken at times. But she is not a woman in relationship to me as a man. I am simply being a thoughtful person who is concerned about his temporary neighbor."

Miriam frowned. "Do tell."

"I'm attempting to do that. I'm telling you that I have no interest in Calico Smith beyond a humanitarian one. You, however, fueled by my mother's enthusiasm for the subject, will convince yourself that there's a romance brewing here, and will envision me bouncing baby Calicos on my knee."

"Oh, how sweet," Miriam said dreamily.

"Miriam, I have every intention of falling in love someday, marrying, and having a family. However, that series of events will not be choreographed by you and my mother."

"That's fine, dear. In the meantime, tell me more about Calico."

Pierce rolled his eyes heavenward. "Give me strength."

Three

At seven o'clock that evening, Pierce mumbled an earthy expletive, then strode across the living room to peer—again—through the small security peephole in the door.

His behavior was ridiculous, he admonished himself, and totally out of character. He didn't spy on his neighbors, for Pete's sake, but there he was boldly spying on his neighbor.

No, now wait a minute, he reasoned. He wasn't nosy, he was . . . he was conducting himself as any concerned human being would, who simply wished to be assured that Calico Smith hadn't passed out from the heat while doing her chicken routine.

Pierce pounded the door once with his fist, then returned to his leather chair and sprawled into it. He drummed his fingers on the arms in a mismatched rhythm, a deep frown on his face.

The minute he'd come home from work he'd

grabbed a bowl and gone next door to do the borrow-a-cup-of-sugar bit with Calico. She hadn't answered his insistent knocking, though, and ever since then he'd been popping up like a pogo stick to look through the peephole.

He was exhausted, and would no doubt suffer a relapse of the flu because he was being such a nice guy. Well, enough was enough, he told himself. He wasn't going over to that door again.

Pierce lunged to his feet and strode to the door.

As he peeked through the hole, he stiffened. Despite the fact that the device was constructed to give a full view of whoever was outside the door, the person strolling by was so incredibly tall, Pierce could only see the man from the neck to the knees.

As the giant moved out of range, Pierce quietly opened the door a few inches, straining to hear. The sound of a rat-a-tat-tat knock reached him, then moments later he heard Calico's voice.

"Hi, Sticks," she said. "Come in and meet Homer."

"All right," Sticks said. "But Homer had better mind his manners, or he's dead meat. You belong only to me, honey pie."

Pierce heard the door close, then all was silent. He shut his own door, his mind racing.

He'd somehow missed Calico's arrival home. And despite his vigil he'd been unaware of Homer entering her apartment too. Now there was a giant named Sticks, who had made it dismally clear that he considered Calico his personal property. What was Calico doing with two men in her apartment?

"It's none of your business, Anderson," he said aloud. He'd done his duty. He was now assured that Calico hadn't fainted from the heat while being a chicken, and that was that.

He walked into the kitchen, chewed a vitamin C tablet, and drank a carefully measured eight ounces of milk. Did Calico drink enough milk? he wondered.

"Dammit," he muttered, plunking the empty glass down on the counter. Why was Calico still taking up space in his mind? Why couldn't he shake her loose, forget her? She was safely home . . . with two jokers named Homer and Sticks.

Calico had about her a sense of innocence, he mused. She wasn't the worldly, streetwise type, not even close. She evoked in a man a desire to protect her, whether that man wanted to feel protective or not.

She was alone with two men at that very minute—one of whom appeared to be a direct descendant of a tree—and there was no telling what might happen over there. Calico was so delicate, so vulnerable and trusting. She'd even asked him, a total stranger, to unstick her head from her body, for heaven's sake.

Pierce shook his head in defeat, then snatched up a bowl big enough to hold an entire five-pound bag of sugar and left the apartment.

• • •

Calico jotted a series of numbers onto a piece of paper, then nodded.

"So far," she called toward the kitchen, "this calculus is perfect, Sticks. I think you're finally getting the hang of it."

"I won't tell you how long it took me to do that page," he answered. "The stuff is Greek. I'm going for a degree in physical education, since it'll be a good career once I retire from pro basketball, and I sure don't see why I need to know calculus. Hey, this popcorn smells great."

"Just don't burn it like you did last time. Shake the pan."

"I'm shakin', I'm shakin'."

"Abby made cheese popcorn once. It was terrific. That Abby is a whiz in the kitchen. Don't you think she's a marvelous cook, Sticks?"

"I've never thought about it, but now that you mention it I guess she does whip up a decent meal. Don't talk to me. You're checking my calculus."

Calico frowned. "Shake the pan."

Darn that Sticks, she thought. What was it going to take to get him to appreciate Abby for the wonderful woman she was? She was pretty, with gorgeous blond hair and blue eyes, was five feet ten, had a fabulous figure, and was intelligent to boot. Sticks dated ditzy basketball groupies when he had the time and treated Abby like a sister, the same way he did Calico. And for that, she'd like to shake Sticks Statler the way he was supposedly shaking the popcorn pan.

A knock at the door brought Calico from her thoughts. She crossed the room and opened the door.

"Pierce," she said, surprised but pleased. "Come in. How are you feeling?" He looked, as usual, utterly devastating. He was wearing khaki pants and a brown knit shirt that did unbelievable things for his wonderful dark eyes. And those eyelashes were there, causing that funny flutter in her stomach. "You look great. I mean, you're not as pale as you were." She paused, telling her body to calm down and her mind to start thinking straight again. "Pierce, would you care to bring your bowl inside?"

"What?" he said, then shook his head. "Oh, yes. Thank you."

He'd forgotten to breathe again, Pierce fumed inwardly as he stepped into the apartment. One look at Calico, Miss Sunshine-Smile Smith, and he was rendered completely immobile. What was it about this little whisper of a woman that threw him so off kilter?

Forget it, he told himself. He was there on a rescue mission, to save Calico from her innocent self, and from the clutches of Sticks the Tree and whoever the miscreant Homer was.

"Do we have company?" a man yelled from the kitchen. "I can handle that. There's enough for everyone."

Good Lord, Pierce thought, his grip on the bowl tightening. The man was a pervert, and was apparently into orgies. This situation was even more serious than he'd thought.

"My neighbor is here," Calico answered. "Pierce Anderson. I'll introduce you when you come out of there with the goodies."

Goodies? Pierce repeated silently.

"Now then," Calico said, smiling at him, "what can I do for your bowl?"

"Oh," he said. "Sugar. I came to borrow sugar. I'm sorry if I interrupted something . . . important. You're obviously very . . . busy."

"Oh, no problem. It used to take Sticks and me half the night, but he's really getting the hang of it now. He still has to work very hard at it, but from what I've seen so far this evening, his efforts are well worth the time spent."

"Ohmigod," Pierce muttered.

"Pardon me?"

"Nothing. Is there anyone else here, Calico?"

She laughed, and once again instantaneous heat coursed through Pierce's body at that happy sound.

"Only Homer," she said. "He's very frisky tonight. I think the picture in the magazine really got him going."

"That's nice," Pierce said weakly.

"Do sit down, Pierce," she said. "Sticks and I really have to get back to it, but we can certainly take a break."

"It?" he asked. "Get back to *it*?"

"Well, yes, the—"

"Perfection," Sticks said, striding into the room carrying a huge bowl. "Goodies galore. The popcorn is outstanding. Not one burned piece, every kernel evenly salted and buttered. I'm telling you, I amaze myself at times." He looked at Pierce. "I'm Sticks Statler."

"Pierce Anderson," he said, staring at the bowl Sticks carried. "That's the goodies? Popcorn?"

"Yeah," Sticks said. "You must have ESP. You brought your own bowl."

"He came to borrow sugar," Calico said. "Let's sit down and dive in. It smells so good. Oh, I'll get some sodas to drink with this."

"I'll do it," Sticks said, setting the bowl on the coffee table. "And napkins. We're going to need napkins because I was very generous with the melted butter." He turned and retraced his steps to the kitchen.

"I wish Homer could have some popcorn," Calico said, sitting down on the sofa. "Poor little guy. Goldfish sure do get the short end of the stick."

"Gold"—Pierce sank onto a flowered chair—"fish?"

"Yes." She pointed across the room. "See? That's Homer."

"Booze and bibs," Sticks said, returning to the living room. He set three cans of soda and a stack of napkins next to the popcorn. "I'm celebrating," he added to Pierce. "This is the first time I've had ten calculus problems in a row figured right. Oh, man, if I've finally gotten the edge on this junk, I'll be one happy guy. When I think of all those hours, those long nights we spent, Calico, I exhaust myself. Calculus was invented by a sadist."

Pierce Anderson laughed.

He leaned back in his chair and fell apart, laughing until tears filled his eyes and he was gasping for breath. Calico and Sticks stared at him in amazement.

"He's flipped his switch," Sticks whispered. "Your flashy architect is bonkers, sweetie pie."

"He's not mine," she whispered back. "And don't be rude. Sticks, people in the wealthy, white-collar world that Pierce lives in must have a different . . . I don't know, sense of humor than we do. There's obviously something extremely amusing going on here, and we're too blue collar to recognize it."

Sticks nodded. "Yeah, I see what you mean. That's rather depressing, isn't it? We don't even know how to laugh rich. I gotta learn this stuff, Calico, for when I'm making big bucks as a pro."

She patted him on the knee. "There's plenty of time for that. You need all your gray matter for your calculus right now." She sighed as she watched Pierce, still chuckling, wipe tears from his eyes. "Doesn't Pierce have a marvelous laugh? It's so deep and full. So male."

"The man is not for you," Sticks said, still whispering. "Calico, his shirt and slacks cost more than Hoop's so-called car."

"*Anything* is worth more than that pile of junk." She sighed again. "But I know what you mean. Pierce is out of my league."

"Hey, you're as good as anyone on this planet,

rosebud. It's just that there are the 'haves' and the 'have-nots.' Someday you and I will belong to the 'have' group, but right now . . ."

"Yes, yes, I understand. Shh. I think he's running out of steam."

"Oh, Lord," Pierce said, splaying one hand on his chest. "I think I strained my lungs. Whew. Listen, I apologize for coming unglued like that. It isn't like me at all. I can't remember when I've laughed so hard. Actually, it felt great, but it was extremely impolite. So, I'm sorry."

"Hey, no sweat," Sticks said, shrugging. "Calico and I missed the joke, but that's cool."

"I think it best if I don't try to explain what set me off," Pierce said.

"That's fine, Pierce," Calico said. She munched on a handful of popcorn. "Mmm. Delicious. It's the best you've ever made, Sticks. Help yourself, Pierce."

He leaned forward and peered into the bowl. "Did you say that's real butter on there?"

"Yep," Sticks said, and shoved some into his mouth.

"Thanks for the offer," Pierce said, "but I'll pass. Butter is very high in cholesterol as well as fat. I've had my quota of each for today." He smiled pleasantly.

"Huh?" Sticks said.

Calico stared at the pile of popcorn in the palm of her hand. "Cholesterol and fat? Well, my goodness, isn't that interesting? I realize there's a great deal of hoopla over cholesterol these days, but I haven't paid much attention."

"You should, Calico," Pierce said seriously. "It has a way of sneaking up on you, and you're in physical trouble before you realize it. Your heart, you know. Cholesterol, fat . . . they head straight for the old ticker. To counter that, I've added oat bran to my diet, and a large daily dosage of niacin." He nodded decisively. "You really ought to consider doing that."

"Weird," Sticks mumbled, reaching for more popcorn.

"I was concerned about you today, Calico," Pierce went on. "It was much hotter than yesterday, and I knew you were in that chicken suit."

"Why, thank you, Pierce," she said. "It was very thoughtful of you to be concerned. It *was* awfully warm, but I survived." She smiled at him. "Thankfully," she added, "this was my last day as a chicken." She continued gazing at him, and her smile slowly faded as she felt herself becoming lost in his dark eyes.

"Good," he said, his gaze intently locked with hers. "The temperature will be climbing steadily from now on, you know. It's going to be getting hotter . . . and . . . hotter . . . and . . ."

"Yes," she murmured. "Much . . . hotter."

Hotter, she thought dazedly. Just like the strange, swirling heat within her. Her heart was beating like a wild drum, and she felt as though his compelling gaze was drawing her toward him, right into his arms. Oh, the effect he had on her was so unsettling. And so wonderful. And so frightening.

Blue as a summer sky, Pierce thought, as he stared at Calico's eyes. Blue as sapphires. Blue as his liquid nighttime cold medication. Such beautiful eyes she had, mesmerizing eyes, that were pinning him in place, and causing a potent heat to coil low in his body. Lord above, what this woman did to him.

Sticks's gaze darted back and forth between Calico and Pierce, then he scowled fiercely.

"Popcorn is getting cold," he said in a voice loud enough to have announced the condition of the snack to a gymnasium full of people.

Both Calico and Pierce jerked in surprise, and the hazy, sensual spell that had fallen over them was broken.

"Well, recess is over," Sticks said. "Time to tackle the old calculus again."

Pierce got to his feet. "I'll be on my way."

Calico shot Sticks a quick glare, then stood up. She retrieved Pierce's bowl from where he'd set it on the coffee table.

"I'll get you some sugar, Pierce," she said.

"Some what?" he asked, blinking in confusion. "Oh, yes, right, my sugar. I came to borrow sugar, didn't I? Sure enough."

Calico started toward the kitchen, and Pierce headed for the front door, well aware that Sticks was close on his heels. When Calico returned, she handed the bowl to Pierce.

"Thank you very much," he said.

"You're very welcome, Pierce."

Sticks flung one long arm across Calico's shoulders and hauled her to his side, nearly lifting her off her feet in the process. He extended his right hand to Pierce.

"Great meeting you, Anderson," he said, vigorously pumping Pierce's hand. "Calico and I always enjoy having company. Right, petunia? You bet. Well, see ya, Pierce."

Calico attempted to wiggle free of Sticks's hold, but realized at once that the effort was useless.

"Good night, Pierce," she said.

"Good night."

He turned and left the apartment, closing the door behind him with a quiet click.

Sticks dropped his arm from Calico's shoulders and produced his biggest, most dazzling smile. Calico narrowed her eyes and planted her fists on her hips.

"What did you think you were doing?" she asked, her voice rising with anger. "What was this 'Calico and I always enjoy having company' spiel? You made it sound as though you and I . . . Sticks Statler, I'd wring your neck if I could reach it."

He raised both hands. "Now, now, stay loose. I was simply doing my job as your big brother, protecting you from Joe Slick. Calico, the man leered at you with lust in his eyes."

"Leered with lust?" she repeated, her tone a notch higher.

"Yep."

She opened her mouth to retort, then snapped it closed. Placing one fingertip on her chin, she stared thoughtfully up at the ceiling.

"Leered with lust," she murmured, and smiled. "Well, fancy that."

"I'm telling you," Sticks said, "you've got to stay away from that guy. He spells nothing but trouble for you. Do you hear me?"

She frowned at her friend. "The whole world can hear you."

"I don't care as long as I'm getting through to your tiny mind. Come on, let's polish off the popcorn, then get back to the calculus."

"I don't want any more popcorn," she said breezily, as they returned to the living room. "One must be careful of one's cholesterol and fat intake, you know."

Sticks said a word that would have earned him a technical foul in a basketball game.

That night, Pierce Anderson dreamed that he was being chased through a dense forest of tall trees that had arms and legs. He could hardly see where he was going after the sky opened and dumped rain that fell in the form of buttered popcorn.

Four

When Calico awoke the next morning, she was immediately aware that she was not her usual peppy, cheerful self.

She yawned, stretched, blinked away the last fogginess of sleep, and realized that she did, indeed, have a hefty case of what Gran would have called, "the blahs and the blues."

Dear, dear Gran, Calico thought. Even though it had been over two years since her grandmother had died peacefully in her sleep, Calico still missed the gentle, loving woman who had raised her.

She pulled the flowered sheet to her chin and stared up at the ceiling.

Gran, Calico knew, would have no patience if she gave in to the blahs and blues and spent the day in a dark, gloomy mood. "Have a talk with yourself," Gran would instruct, "and find out what's troubling you, child. Then either fix it or accept things as they are. But smile. No matter what, Calico Smith, smile."

Calico sighed. She didn't want to smile, darn it. And she also, she admitted, was pouting, and would much prefer just to trudge her way through the day without a smile in sight.

But she knew she'd feel Gran tapping her on the shoulder, insisting that Calico follow the rules set down since childhood.

"So, okay," she said to the silent room, "what is your problem, Miss Smith?"

Miss Smith, her mind echoed. *Miss,* not *Mrs.* She was Calico, alone, and for the first time that she could remember, she felt lonely.

"Well, for Pete's sake," she muttered, and sat up on the edge of the bed.

Of course she was alone, she reasoned. She had a mission, a goal, that did not allow room for more than work, study, and a few close friends. She knew that, but . . . Well, there seemed to be a void, an empty space, in her life that she'd never noticed before.

She propped her elbows on her knees and plunked her chin in her hands.

A man, her mind whispered. Her blahs and blues were caused by a yearning for a special man, someone who would be there with her through the good days and bad. Someone to laugh with, cry with, share the glorious and the mundane with.

Someone to love, heart, mind, body, and soul, and who would love her in kind.

Calico's eyes widened and she straightened as

stiff as a board. There, appearing so real in her mind that she might reach out and touch him, was the image of Pierce Anderson. Tall and handsome, eyelashes, handkerchief, and all, Pierce stood smiling at Calico.

She jumped to her feet and flapped her hands at the illusion.

"Shoo, shoo. Go away, Pierce Anderson. I don't have time for you. Besides, you're the wrong man. You're out of my league, so get out of my head."

The mirage refused to budge.

Calico inched her way along the edge of the bed, then dashed for her suitcase, which was propped open against the wall. She snatched up clean underwear, grabbed jeans and a red- and white-checked blouse from the closet, then ran into the bathroom and slammed the door behind her.

She was an idiot, she admonished herself, when she stood under the hot water in the shower. She'd behaved as though Pierce had actually been in her bedroom. Had he been leering with lust? No, he'd been smiling with smoldering desire radiating from the depths of his eyes.

"Calico, shut up your brain."

As she dried herself with the enormous towel and then dressed, she lectured herself sternly on the facts—she was not lonely, it simply wasn't her turn yet for a serious relationship, and the blahs and blues would just have to shuffle off to Buffalo.

She also tacked on, as she brushed her hair, that there would be no further daydreaming about Pierce, nor would he, imaginary or real, be allowed to reappear in her bedroom. And that, thank you very much, was that.

With a smile that would have made Gran proud firmly in place, Calico ate breakfast, packed her tote bag, and fed Homer. She propped another magazine open next to the goldfish's bowl, today's picture being one of a sweeping cornfield in Iowa, and left the apartment.

Smiling.

But when she stepped into the elevator, the bright smile slid right off her chin as she met the gaze of Pierce Anderson.

"Oh . . . I . . . Well . . ." she mumbled, dragging her gaze down to focus on the knot of his tie. "Hi. Are you feeling well? You look great. Yes, you—you certainly do. Great." She nodded. "Fit as a fiddle. So! Good morning, Pierce. Would you press the button, please? I'm going down. Of course I am. Why on earth would I be going in any direction but down? Oh, Calico, shut up. Please just shut up."

"Calico," he said, "are you in love with the tree? I mean, with Sticks?"

What? Pierce thought incredulously. Had he really asked her that? Had he opened his big mouth and actually asked her that? He hadn't realized he'd even been wondering about it, let alone have the question spill out all over the elevator. Oh, good Lord, what was the matter with him? Maybe his vitamin B was chemically warring with his vitamin A and scrambling his brain waves. Or maybe—

"Am I in love with Sticks?" she repeated, bringing him back to attention.

Say yes, Calico told herself. Almost everyone she knew at Arizona State University believed she and Sticks were in love. If Pierce thought that was the situation, he'd stay out of her way. He'd quickly become out of sight, out of mind, and her problem of him taking up her brain space would be solved. All she had to do was answer yes.

"No," she heard herself say.

"No?"

"Sticks and I are very close friends, like a brother and sister," she rattled on. "Chums, buddies, you know what I mean?"

Fantastic, Pierce thought, elated. That was terrific news. That was what he'd been hoping to hear because—No, dammit, it was terrible.

A section of his scrambled brain was ecstatic about the fact that Calico was not involved with Sticks. But another part was totally confused over his spontaneous reaction of joy, and that was producing waves of . . . What was it? Fear? Lord, yes, fear, real fear, that Calico was unattached.

Why? Pierce asked himself. What was he afraid of? Granted, each time he'd been with her Calico had thrown him off kilter, caused him to behave like a schoolboy. To gaze into her blue eyes was to feel the undeniable heat of desire tighten throughout his body.

He'd worried about her health when he'd imagined her becoming an ill, overheated chicken.

He'd dashed to her door like an idiot when he'd thought she'd been trapped by her own innocence and vulnerability by Sticks and Homer.

He'd dreamed of her at night, daydreamed about her in his waking hours.

She was driving him crazy, and he wanted it stopped. Calico was lovely, as refreshing as a spring breeze, but she wasn't his type. She simply didn't fit the picture in his mind of the woman he hoped to find and marry. Somehow, he had to sever once and for all the sensual threads she wove around him.

"Pierce?" she said. "You're still pressing the button to hold the door open."

"What? Oh, yes, so I am. Do you have an early class to get to?"

"No, not this morning. I was going to the library to study, then I have a student to tutor at eleven. Tutoring is one of my many odd jobs." She gazed bemusedly at him. "Why did you ask me about Sticks?"

"I . . . Look, let's go someplace for a cup of coffee, okay? I'll drive you over to the campus later."

"Why?"

"Why? Because coffee is what most people

drink in the morning. I limit myself to two cups a day. I've only had one so far today, so . . ."

She shrugged. "It's fine with me. We'll have a cup of coffee. You still haven't told me why you asked about Sticks, though. Is it because you're just basically nosy?"

He glared at her, then released the button that had kept the door open and pressed the one that would whiz them to the underground garage. He performed his handkerchief-over-his-nose-and-mouth routine in the garage, and they were soon caught up in the surging traffic on Scottsdale Road.

When they stopped at a red light, he pressed one thumb between his eyebrows.

"Stress headache," he said. "I'm suffering from stress. See what you do to me, Calico Smith?"

"Me?" she said, splaying one hand on her chest. "*I'm* causing you stress?"

"Damn right."

"That's absurd. I haven't done anything unusual. I've been minding my own business, just being me."

The traffic light turned green, and Pierce sped along the road.

"Exactly," he said. "It's you being you that is doing this." He narrowed his eyes. "Maybe I should look into the practice of meditation, or take up yoga. Stress is a physically and mentally depleting state. I want you to know that I really resent this, Calico."

She folded her arms across her breasts and glowered out the windshield.

"This is," she said, "the most ridiculous conversation I've ever taken part in. No, forget that. It's not a conversation because I refuse to address another word you're saying. This is a sermonette delivered by you that doesn't make any sense."

"Mmm," he said, and to Calico it sounded like a growl. "There's a coffee shop up ahead."

No more words were spoken as they entered the café and were shown to a booth. Pierce ordered coffee and oat bran muffins for them both.

"Did it ever occur to you, Mr. Anderson," Calico asked coolly as the waitress walked away, "that I might not like oat bran muffins?"

"They're good for you," he said. "Lord knows you need something healthy in your system after all that buttered popcorn you ate last night."

Calico rolled her eyes heavenward.

A few minutes later, the waitress returned with a plate of muffins and filled their coffee cups. Calico ignored the muffins, despite the fact that they looked delicious. Pierce ate one, sipped his coffee, then leaned back in the booth and sighed.

"Calico," he said quietly, "we have a problem." He sat forward again and folded his arms on the top of the table. "Well, maybe you don't, but I do."

"What kind of problem?" she asked, wrapping her hands around her coffee cup.

"Well, for some unknown reason I find myself very preoccupied by you. I keep wondering if you're all right, what you're doing, that sort of thing."

Hooray! Calico's mind cheered. No, no, she told herself instantly. That was the wrong reaction.

"You don't seem very pleased about it," she said. "No, obviously you're not, because you've labeled it a problem. I . . . I find myself thinking a lot about you, too, Pierce. And I agree that it's a problem, a very annoying situation."

"Annoying?" he said. "Thinking about me is annoying? Thanks a helluva lot. I'm a very nice person, Calico Smith. To say that the thought of me is annoying is extremely rude."

"No worse than your announcing that I'm a problem," she said, with an indignant sniff. "Pierce, this is not a fun way to start the day. May we go, please?"

"No," he said. "We have to talk this through."

She sighed. "Fine. You have the floor. You also have muffins to eat because I think they look gross."

"Forget the muffins. Calico, we've both admitted that we're reacting—or maybe overreacting—to each other. There wouldn't be anything wrong with that except . . ." His voice trailed off.

"Except that we're not really suited to each other," she said softly. "I mean, you're a man and I'm a woman, and that part is dandy. But on a social scale we don't match up at all. Oh, you could say that that sort of thing doesn't matter anymore, but it does, it really does. You're tuxedo and champagne, and I'm jeans and beer. Those are very different worlds, Pierce, and they don't mesh. I understand that."

"No, now wait a minute," he said. "I confess that I did think when we first met that you weren't my type, or I wasn't your type. But hearing you spell it out like that sounds terrible. It sounds snobbish and extremely ridiculous." He straightened and smiled. "I apologize, Calico. You're not a problem, you're a—a happening, an experience."

"Pierce . . ."

He reached across the table and grasped her hands. As he gazed into her eyes, his smile faded.

Calico swallowed heavily, feeling as though an entire oat bran muffin was stuck in her throat. Her heart pounded, and a shiver coursed through her even as she was aware of the incredible heat emanating from Pierce's strong hands.

And then . . . Oh, Lord have mercy. He was stroking his thumb back and forth across her hand in a steady rhythm that was matched by a pulsing sensation low and deep within her.

Calico, she told herself, it's only a thumb. A thumb that was attached to Pierce's hand, that was connected to his body, that . . . Great, she thought. Any minute now she'd burst into the song about the thighbone connected to the hipbone, or however that ditty went. And if she gave one more second of thought to Pierce's thigh, she'd end up leaping across the table and plopping herself on his lap.

She had to snatch her hands back, she decided. And she would . . . in a minute. She had to stop gazing into the mesmerizing depths of his gorgeous eyes, which were framed by those incredible eyelashes. And she would . . . in a minute. She had to put emotional distance between herself and Pierce, not listen to his declaration that she was "a happening." And she would . . . after one more teeny-tiny minute.

Sighing silently, Calico slowly and reluctantly slid her hands from beneath Pierce's and laced her fingers together on her lap. She tore her gaze from his eyes, stared at his chin—oh, what a beautifully masculine chin—and straightened her shoulders.

"Pierce," she said, praying her voice was steady, "I don't know where this discussion is headed, but I have no intention of being a happening or an experience. That plunks me into a category as appealing as eating sushi for the first time. Why don't you just gobble up your oat bran muffins so we can leave?"

"No, Calico, this is important. No one has ever unsettled me the way you do. I want to know what this is, where it might be headed."

"I'm not a new brand of vitamin pill to be checked out, Pierce Anderson," she said, narrowing her eyes. "This is edging toward insulting."

"It's exciting, not insulting. Don't you want to know why you've been thinking about me a great deal, Calico?"

Oh, yes, she thought dreamily. She wanted to explore all kinds of avenues in connection with Pierce. But she had no intention of doing that.

She leaned toward him and looked directly into his eyes again. "Aha!" she said, and nodded decisively. "Sticks was right. You're leering at me with lust."

"I am not," he said, much too loudly. He glanced around, and lowered his voice when he spoke again. "What you must be seeing in my eyes is desire, not lust. You *are* a very desirable woman, Calico, and refreshing, and lovely, and full of a zest for life. I've never met anyone like you before.

"Okay," he went on, "I had a preconceived image in my mind of the type of woman I would eventually marry, but I'm flexible. I can't let you just disappear from my life without pursuing whatever may, or may not, be between us. You're an intelligent woman. I have to believe that you want the answers to these questions as much as I do."

"What I want, Pierce," she said, sinking back against the booth, "is to be a CPA. I have tunnel vision about that. I've worked very hard for a very long time, and I'm close to achieving that goal. No one is going to keep me from accomplishing that."

"Well, sure, I know that you—"

"Listen to me," she interrupted. "Please, just listen for a minute. I don't have time to be involved with a man, to pursue what you see as a fascinating mystery between us. Even if I did have time, I wouldn't do it because our worlds are so far apart, there wouldn't be any point in it."

"That's nonsense."

"No, it isn't, Pierce. You're one of the 'haves,' I'm a 'have not.' I get the feeling that things have always come easily for you. You set your goals, obtained them, and that was that. Did it ever occur to you that I popped into your life when you were rather bored? You needed a change, some zing in your existence, so you've decided to hang out with a chicken for a while. No, thank you, I'll pass."

"You're twisting everything around," he said, frowning. "You make it sound as though I'm playing games to break the monotony of my routine. You're wrong. I'm very serious about everything I've said."

"So am I, so end of story. I have to get to the campus. If you want to stay and enjoy your oat bran, I'll catch a bus."

"Dammit, Calico, you're not being fair. Why are you being so stubborn about this?"

"Stubborn? I'm not stubborn, I'm surviving. I'm doing what I have to do to accomplish my goals. It's just one of a multitude of examples of how different we are, how far apart our worlds are. Don't stand in judgment of me until you've walked in my shoes, Pierce. The thing is, it's very apparent that you'll never have shoes like mine, nor move through life on the path I have to take."

She slid out of the booth. "It was nice meeting you," she said quietly, "but there's nothing more to say on the subject. I'm walking out of here to catch a bus. Please don't make a scene by charging after me. It's better this way. It's over before it's really begun. Good-bye, Pierce Anderson."

With that, she turned and hurried out of the café.

Pierce watched her go, then reached into the inside pocket of his suit coat. He withdrew the small yellow feather he'd found on his living room floor the day Calico had been a chicken.

He stroked the feather with his thumb, staring in the direction Calico had gone, then carefully returned the feather to his pocket.

As he reached for another oat bran muffin, he was smiling.

Five

"So," Calico said, "there you have it, Abby. I left that café this morning and . . . The thing I can't understand is why I've had the blahs and the blues all day. Still have them, in fact. I mean, cripes, it's not as though Pierce Anderson and I had had a long affair that just ended. It's not as though we were in love with each other. Heavenly days, I hardly know the man."

Abby Kolb stretched her long jean-clad legs out on the flowered sofa and frowned at Calico.

"Well," she said, "there are times when you meet someone special whom you instantly feel like you've known forever. Something just sort of clicks. Looking back, I think it was about three seconds after I said, 'How do you do?' to Sticks that I realized I was a goner. You can't dismiss Pierce on the basis of how many hours, or days, you've known him."

"Oh." Calico studied the original painting on

the opposite wall as she mulled that over. "Well, there are enough other reasons why Pierce is the wrong man for me. Facts are facts, I understand that, but I swear if anyone looked at me crooked right now, I'd burst into tears. This is so absurd."

"I think it's wonderful. I wish Sticks thought I was a happening. He either acts as though I'm invisible, or I'm his sister or something. But we're not talking about me."

"Yes, we are," Calico said, "because I don't want to discuss me and Pierce any further." She turned her head to gaze at the goldfish. "Hi, Homer, how's life?"

"Homer is a cute fish," Abby said. "Do you realize that we know a goldfish who lives in a swanky apartment? You and I rent matchbook-size rooms in a crummy old house, and Homer is a Scottsdale goldfish."

Calico laughed. "Who would have thought we'd know a fish who was higher on the social scale than us?"

Abby frowned again. "I wish you'd cut that out. People are people, Calico. Maybe we're broke right now, but it won't always be this way. You're going to become a CPA. I'm about to graduate with a degree in computer science. But I'd still think we were as good as the next guy if all we did was work at a fast-food place forever. I knew your grandmother, remember? I never heard her talk about class distinction or social status. Where did you get this attitude?"

Calico shrugged. "Probably in school as I grew

up. I can't remember a time when I wasn't aware that in this supposedly democratic country of ours there are very real class distinctions." She frowned as some particularly painful memories reared their ugly heads. "Kids can be cruel when the mood strikes," she went on, almost to herself. "I always had secondhand clothes that weren't the current style, and the other girls . . . I didn't say anything to Gran because I knew she was doing the best she could. My parents left a pile of bills and me, a three-month-old baby, when they were killed in that car accident."

"Calico, we're not living in Victorian England here. No one is going to look down their nose and say, 'Tsk, tsk, Pierce Anderson is involved with a chicken who is not of the upper crust.' You've got to get your act together about this stuff."

"Abby, there's more to it than that. Okay, maybe I'm too sensitive about social standing. I'll have to give that some thought. But there's still the fact that I have no time for Pierce, or any man. I'm so close to achieving my goal, but I still have to find a job, pay back my student loans. No, I have to stay on track or I'll blow the whole thing."

"So you're brushing off Pierce."

"I have to. I just wish I knew why I'm so—so sad about it. Oh, forget it. Let's have some ice cream, then we'll hit the books. I'm glad you're spending the night here. Mrs. Weatherby said I was more than welcome to have a friend in."

Abby followed her into the kitchen and watched as Calico retrieved a gallon of ice cream from the freezer.

"What is this stuff?" Abby asked, peering at the label on the carton.

"No fat, no cholesterol ice milk," Calico said, reaching into the cupboard for bowls. "Pierce says we have to watch our intake of fat and cholesterol because it can sneak up on our tickers and gum up the works."

"How fascinating," Abby said, stifling a laugh. "Pierce says all that, huh?"

"Oh, yes." She took two spoons out of a drawer. "Abby, have you ever thought about the potential danger in inhaling exhaust fumes? And buses. They're the absolute worst culprits as far as polluting the air with exhaust fumes. Pierce says . . ."

As Calico chattered on, Abby stared at her friend, deep in thought.

The next morning, Pierce stood with his front door open a fraction of an inch, his ear close to the minuscule opening between the door and the frame. He'd been standing in that unnatural, uncomfortable position for over half an hour and would, he supposed, have to investigate the possibility of visiting a chiropractor to straighten out his aching back. Spines out of line could cause a domino-theory series of ailments.

Suddenly he tensed as he heard the sound of feminine laughter floating down the hall.

Yes, he thought, that was the tinkling resonance of Calico's laugh. He'd know it anywhere, as did his body, which was at once tautening as fierce desire swept through him.

He listened for two more beats of his racing heart, then snatched up his briefcase and sauntered out of the apartment. He yawned as he went, deciding it added a nice touch of nonchalance.

"Oh, well, hello," he said, an expression of great surprise on his face as he spotted Calico and another woman. "Good morning, Calico." He shifted his gaze to the other woman. "I'm Pierce Anderson. And you are?"

"Abby Kolb," she said, grinning broadly. "I'm Calico's best friend. I can't tell you what a pleasure this is. I've heard so much about you, Pierce. Just oodles and oodles."

Calico grabbed Abby's arm. "Come on," she said, avoiding looking directly into Pierce's eyes. "We're going to miss the bus, Abby."

"Well, my goodness, Calico," Abby said, refusing to budge. "After what you told me about exhaust fumes, I'm not sure we should ride the bus."

A wide smile broke across Pierce's face as he looked at Calico.

"You told Abby what I said about exhaust fumes?" he asked.

Calico fiddled with the middle button on her blue cotton blouse. Her expression of concentration gave the impression that the button was the most interesting thing she'd ever seen.

"It may have come up in passing conversation," she said, shrugging.

"It wasn't passing," Abby said. "It was an entire paragraph. You remember, Calico, it was when we were serving up our no fat, no cholesterol ice milk."

"Oh, good night," Calico muttered, feeling a warm flush stain her cheeks.

"You ate . . ." Pierce's smile grew even bigger. "What flavor?"

"I don't recall," Calico said to the button.

"Natural fruit," Abby said. "Pure, unadulterated natural fruit. Delicious."

"Ab-by," Calico said through clenched teeth, "we are going to be late for class."

"Then let's all hop into the elevator, shall we?" Abby said cheerfully, and started off down the hall again.

"Hop?" Calico echoed.

Pierce chuckled. "She must have forgotten that you're a chicken, not a rabbit."

Do not look at this man, Calico silently directed herself. Hop down the hall, get into the elevator, and disappear. Do not look at Pierce Anderson.

She lifted her head and met Pierce's gaze.

Oh, damn, she thought.

Oh, yes, he thought.

Sapphire-blue eyes and chocolate-brown eyes locked together as exploding sensations rocketed through one male body, tall and taut, and one female body, small and soft. Heat pulsed, churned, and swirled, the heat of desire, not lust, and it seemed to crackle through the air.

"Calico," Pierce said, his head bending down toward hers.

"Yoo-hoo," Abby called as she poked her head out of the elevator. "Oh, nice timing, Abby," she mumbled to herself in the next breath. "I'd bet my last dime that he was about to kiss her. Blast."

Pierce and Calico jerked to attention when they heard Abby, then turned and marched toward the elevator, looking to Abby like a couple of windup toys. They stepped into the elevator, and Abby pressed the necessary buttons.

Pierce glanced at both women, looking slightly bemused. "I'd offer you both a ride to campus," he said, "but my car only holds two people." He frowned. "I never realized how inefficient that vehicle is."

"I wouldn't say that," Abby said. "It sounds rather cozy. Two is a nice number. It makes me think of tea for two, two becoming a couple, together, one and one makes two, and—"

"Abby," Calico said, "put a cork in it."

"Gotcha."

The elevator bumped to a gentle stop, and the doors swished open. Calico whizzed out.

" 'Bye, Pierce," she said, not breaking stride.

"I'll talk to you later, Pierce," Abby whispered. "I have a plan." She left the elevator, saying loudly. "Ta-ta, Pierce. It was enchanting meeting you." She waved good-bye and hurried after Calico.

"See ya," Pierce murmured as both women disappeared out the front doors of the building.

Seeing the stormy expression on Calico's face, Abby decided that since she valued her life, it was best to keep silent during the bus ride to ASU. When they got off at their stop, Calico said good-bye to Abby and started to walk away.

"Hey, wait a minute," Abby said.

Calico stopped and turned, raising her eyebrows. "Yes, Abby?"

"Don't forget about tonight. This is Friday, remember? You and I are meeting Sticks for the poetry reading at The Blue Banana."

"Oh, yes, of course. I'll come to the house, and we'll walk over together. There's no sense in my going back to Scottsdale first. I'll use the extra time to study before we go."

"Okay."

"Abby . . . about Pierce."

"Yes?"

Calico sighed. "Nothing. Forget I said his name. There's just nothing more to say about Pierce Anderson." She turned and walked slowly away.

Abby narrowed her eyes as she watched her go. "We'll just see about that, Miss Smith. Abby Kolb is leaping into action."

Just before eight o'clock that night, Pierce stood on the sidewalk in front of a house that was painted bright blue. A neon sign done in script lettering glowed the announcement that this was "The Blue Banana."

The house was several blocks away from the campus and had, Pierce surmised, been part of a rezoning ordinance. All of the old frame houses along the short street contained some sort of commercial business, but none, to Pierce's eyes, looked quite as . . . interesting as The Blue Banana. Abby had told him when she'd called that afternoon that it was a popular coffeehouse frequented by the ASU students.

During his days at ASU, he mused, he hadn't gone near this type of place. His social life had consisted of sports events, symphonies, live theater, and small parties where stimulating conversation took place.

He eyed The Blue Banana with distaste. It would, no doubt, be crowded, smoky, and noisy. Too many sweaty people would be crammed into too small an area. He did *not* want to go inside The Blue Banana, but he *did* want to see Calico Smith. So . . .

It was certainly understandable, he reasoned, that he wasn't thrilled about an evening spent at an off-campus coffeehouse dump. He was, after all, many years older than most ASU students. His social life consisted of sports events, symphonies, live theater, and small parties where stimulating conversation took place.

Pierce frowned. Well, that was interesting, he thought. He hadn't changed his leisure time activities since his college days. That statement had a disturbingly boring ring to it. He'd fallen into a set pattern of living years before, and hadn't deviated one iota from it since.

Until now. Until Calico. Until he'd opened his apartment door and found himself face-to-face with a human-size chicken, who was turning his well-ordered life upside down and inside out.

Oh, yes, Miss Calico Smith was having a tremendous impact on him. She was, indeed, a happening, and he fully intended to discover just what his sexual and emotional reactions to her meant. Maybe it was something, maybe it was nothing, but he needed to know. So there he was, actually about to walk into an uninviting building with the ridiculous name of The Blue Banana.

He shook his head, strode up the narrow, cracked concrete walkway, and entered the building.

"Abby," Calico said, "why are you wiggling around in your chair like that? You haven't sat still since we got here."

"What?" Abby asked, craning her neck to look over Calico's head. "Can't hear you because of the noise."

"She said," Sticks said loudly, "why are you acting as though you have ants in your pants?"

Abby glared at Sticks. "A gentleman does not make reference to a lady's pants, Mr. Statler."

He grinned. "I didn't ask you if I could get into

them, or whisk them off your luscious body. I was only inquiring about the ants."

She continued to glower at the basketball player. "You wouldn't recognize a luscious body if it landed right in your lap."

"Oh, yeah?" He sat up straighter in his chair. "That's a really stupid thing to say, Abby Kolb. I'm very aware that *you* have a luscious body. As a matter of fact, I've been cognizant . . . " He paused to grin again and say, "Great word, huh? I just learned it . . . cognizant of your physical attributes for a long time. Just because I'm tall doesn't mean that the air is so thin up here, my gray matter is depleted. You do, indeed, have an extremely luscious body."

"Well," Calico said, smiling, "fancy that. Abby, your mouth is open. Say thank you to Sticks for the lovely compliment."

"Thank you, Sticks," Abby said, her gaze riveted to his face, "for the lovely compliment."

"You're welcome." He smiled at her. "I really mean it, Abby. You're a sensational-looking girl."

"Woman," Abby said.

He nodded. "Right, woman. You . . . are . . . definitely . . . a woman." He blinked. "An older woman."

"What?" Abby exclaimed. "A what?"

"A what?" Calico echoed.

"Well, it's true." Sticks looked at Calico, then back at Abby. "You guys are both older than I am."

"I'm eleven months and four days older than you are," Abby said.

He shrugged. "I rest my case."

She stared at him. "Are you telling me that eleven months and four days is a big deal? Are you crazy? Has someone been bouncing a basketball on your brain?"

"Hey," Sticks said, "you're a senior, I'm a junior. I figure that you consider me a cute—tall, but cute—little brother. And Calico . . . Well, jeez, she's twenty-three."

"Gosh," Calico said dryly, "I'm teetering on the edge of senility."

"Sticks," Abby said, "I don't consider you a cute, tall little brother."

"No?" He frowned. "I thought I was cute. A lot of girls . . . women . . . tell me I'm cute. Well, you have the right to your opinion, I guess."

Abby planted her palms flat on the small wobbly table and leaned toward Calico.

"I'm going to kill him, Calico," she said, "with my bare hands. He's not worth going to jail for, but I can't hold myself back. Will you visit me in prison?"

"I certainly will," Calico said. "I'll bring you peanut butter chocolate chip cookies. Go ahead and murder the jerk."

"What did I do?" Sticks asked, pressing one very large hand over his heart. "What in the hell did I do?"

"You're guilty of doing nothing, you idiot," Abby said, with an indignant sniff.

"Huh?"

"Don't speak to me." She suddenly stiffened, her eyes widening. "Well, my, my, look who just came in the door. As I live and breathe, it's Pierce Anderson." She stood up and waved one arm in the air. "Pierce, yoo-hoo, Pierce, over here."

"Oh, good night," Calico said, "you can't be serious. Pierce wouldn't come to The Blue Banana."

"Hi," Pierce said, appearing next to the table.

"You came to The Blue Banana?" Calico asked, wondering where that funny little squeak in her voice had come from.

"Sure," he said. "Why not?"

"Steal a chair and join us," Abby said. "Sticks, move your bony knees. You're taking up more than your share of space under the table."

"Where would you suggest I put them?" Sticks asked.

She narrowed her eyes. "Don't tempt me to answer that. My mother raised me to be a lady."

"You certainly are crabby tonight, Abby Kolb," Sticks said.

Pierce found a chair and managed to squeeze it and himself between Calico and Abby.

"So," he said, glancing around, "it's incredibly smoky in here, isn't it? And crowded. And noisy." He looked down. "Is this stuff on the floor supposed to be sawdust? I think it's seaweed. I bet the fire marshal doesn't know how many people are crowded in here."

Abby kicked him under the table.

"Ow! And it's a great place," he added quickly.

"The bar is certainly unique, isn't it? It's very clever to put two doors on cinder blocks, leaving the doorknobs in place for a stunning artistic touch. And see that? Instead of a mirror behind the bar like you'd expect there's just a large paper sign that says 'Mirror.' We're talking about superior imagination here." He smiled brightly. "Yes, sir, there's nothing like spending a Friday night at The Blue Banana."

Calico stared at him as though she'd never seen him before in her life.

Pierce was there, she thought incredulously. Spouting complete nonsense, but he was there, and was actually smiling as he sat in the smoky, noisy, crowded, germ-laden Blue Banana. Oh, yes, he was certainly there, looking magnificent in a red knit shirt and dark slacks, eyelashes at the ready, one of his legs pressing against hers and causing an incredible heat to swirl throughout her entire body.

Pierce was there and—and Abby had propped one elbow on the minuscule table, rested her chin in her hand, and was gazing at him with a dreamy expression on her face. A dreamy expression? Abby? But Abby was in love with Sticks, so why was she looking at Pierce as though she'd like to gobble him up for dessert?

"So, Abby," Pierce said, still smiling to beat the band, "what are you taking at ASU?"

"I'm graduating in a couple of weeks with a degree in computer science . . ." She fluttered her eyelashes. ". . . Pierce."

Sticks reached over and jiggled Abby's arm, and her chin slipped off her hand.

"Do you have something in your eye, Abby?" he asked.

"No, I don't have something in my eye," she said, shooting him a dark look.

"Drinks, folks?" a gum-chewing young woman asked, appearing by Pierce's elbow.

Calico, Abby, and Sticks ordered colas, and Pierce asked for a glass of mineral water.

"Mineral water?" the waitress repeated. "We have water from a faucet, or I could bring you a bunch of ice cubes. Pick your poison, sport."

"Club soda," Pierce said, "with a twist of lemon."

"This isn't the lounge at the Hilton," the woman said, "but I'll dig around and see if we have a lemon I can twist."

Pierce immediately turned back to Abby as the waitress disappeared into the crowd. "Computers," he said. "That's fascinating, Abby. My secretary does all the office paperwork on a computer, but I don't even know how to turn the thing on."

"I'd be delighted to teach you," Abby said, smiling. "I could help you fully understand the term 'user friendly.'"

"That's extremely nice of you, Abby," Pierce said.

It wasn't nice, Calico thought. It was nauseating. She'd never seen Abby act like this, all flirty, and coy, and—and leering with lust. Abby Kolb was making a play for Pierce Anderson.

Calico's Pierce. What a rotten thing for her best girlfriend to do. It was really shabby.

Now, wait, Calico admonished herself, that wasn't fair. She'd told Abby that she, Calico, had no time, nor space, in her life for Pierce. That declaration made Pierce and his eyelashes available to any interested woman. But Abby? What about Abby's feelings for Sticks?

"Not everyone can get the hang of computers," Sticks said at that moment. "Abby is a superbrain. I was telling Hoop Henderson that just the other day. I said, 'Hoop, that Abby Kolb is not only beautiful, but she's smart too.' Yep, that's what I told Hoop."

Abby's head snapped around, and she stared at Sticks.

"You really said that, Sticks?" she asked, then frowned. "Then, I suppose you tacked on, 'for an older woman, that is.' Right? You probably said I was very intelligent and not bad looking for a senior citizen."

"No," Sticks said thoughtfully, "your age never crossed my mind at the time."

"What's wrong with Abby's age?" Pierce asked, but no one paid any attention to him.

"Eleven months and four days means nothing, Sticks," Abby said, gazing directly into his eyes. "Nothing."

"Yeah, well . . ." Sticks swallowed heavily. "Maybe you're right about that. I mean, you *are* right about that."

"I know," Abby said.

"Bingo," Pierce said. He grinned and looked at Calico.

"Bingo?" she echoed.

"It's good to see you, Calico," he said, his grin fading. "Not that anyone can see too clearly in here because of the smoke, but—"

"Whoa," she said, holding up one hand. "Back up to bingo. Why do I get the feeling that a diabolical plot is unfolding here?"

Pierce laughed. "Diabolical plot? That's rich."

No, Calico thought, Pierce was rich, and she was stone broke. Pierce had decided she was a happening, an experience, and Abby had stepped in like a cruise director and taken charge. Abby's flirting with Pierce had been a ploy to jangle Sticks and Calico, jar them into action. Sticks was falling for it hook, line, and sinker. But Calico Smith was not!

"Here's your drinks," the waitress said, thudding glasses onto the table.

Next to Pierce's glass, she plunked a whole lemon. Pierce reached for his wallet, placed a bill on the woman's tray, then stared at the rather lopsided lemon. Abby and Sticks, who were talking in hushed tones, their heads close together, were oblivious to anything taking place around them.

"What am I supposed to do with that?" Pierce asked, still staring at the lemon.

"Twist it, sweetheart," the waitress said, and walked away.

"I can't believe this," Pierce said. He poked the lemon with one finger.

"What I can't believe," Calico said, leaning toward him, "is that you and Abby actually planned this performance. I'd bet the farm that you've never been in The Blue Banana before in your life. But here you are, inhaling secondary smoke, so Abby could leer with lust at you. Sticks was supposed to come out of the ether and realize that he cared for Abby, which he obviously has done. And me? Oh, well, just push my buttons and have me get jealous as all get-out. What was next? I was supposed to agree with the 'we're a happening' routine? I was supposed to succumb to your gorgeous eyelashes and become putty in your hands?"

"Calico, calm down," he said. "You'll increase your heart rate, which could cause you to hyperventilate. You'll take in more stale smoke if you do, and that's very bad for your health."

"*You*, sir, are hazardous to my health," she said stiffly. "I really resent—"

"Ladies and gentlemen, and the rest of you," a male voice boomed from the microphone on the small stage, interrupting Calico's tirade. "Welcome to The Blue Banana. Tonight you are in for a real treat. We are honored to present Socrates, who will recite his newest brilliant poem, 'Ode to a Grapefruit.' Let's hear a big round of applause for . . . Socrates!"

"'Ode to a Grapefruit'?" A near-hysterical giggle burst from Calico's throat. "Recited at The Blue Banana? If we stay here long enough, we'll have a whole salad."

As the crowd clapped, whistled, and pounded

on the tables, a tall bearded man swept onto the stage clad in a flowing white robe. Calico absently decided that it was a bed sheet, probably percale.

Socrates settled onto a high wooden stool as a circle of light spotlighted him, and smoothed his robe. He appeared to be in his mid-fifties, and his hair and beard were generously sprinkled with gray.

"The grapefruit," he began in a deep, rumbling voice. A hush fell over the audience. "Round. Yellow. Misunderstood. So sadly misunderstood."

Abby and Sticks came out of their huddle and stared at the stage. Pierce shifted in his chair for a better view of the poet, while Calico stared in disbelief.

"The grapefruit," Socrates went on. "Not cherished as it is. Sugar, sugar, sugar, hiding its natural worth. Adornment before acceptance. A tragic symbol of the nature of man."

"Oh, for crying out loud," Calico whispered.

"Shh," Pierce said. "The man has a point."

"He does?"

Socrates raised his arms and spread them wide. Calico saw a small square tag attached to one edge of his toga, and mused that it was the washing instructions for a percale sheet.

"Speak to us, oh so forlorn grapefruit," Socrates boomed. The microphone screeched in protest. "Tell us the error of our ways. Teach us acceptance without adornment before it's too late."

His arms fell heavily to his sides, and he shook his head.

"No, it *is* too late. Man is doomed, unable, unwilling, to hear the voice of the mighty and wise grapefruit, who could save us from ourselves. We continue our quest for more, for sugar, sugar, sugar, for adornment to assure acceptance. We are lost in the rubble. The grapefruit's voice is stilled in death."

Socrates dropped his chin to his chest. The crowd was totally silent. The poet rose and swished off the stage, the sheet billowing around him.

Pierce jumped to his feet and applauded. "Hear, hear," he yelled. "Bravo!"

"Huh?" Calico stared up at Pierce, wide-eyed.

The crowd came alive, clapping loudly, hooting, hollering Socrates's name. The spotlight dimmed, diminished in size, then went out. Everyone turned their attention back to what they'd been doing, the buzz of voices once more filling the room.

Pierce sank back into his chair. "Amazing. That was incredible. What a deep, important social message that man delivered."

"He did?" Sticks asked. "What now? We all charge out and buy grapefruits to see if they want to tell us something? Ol' Socrates probably gets a kickback from the grapefruit growers. Why doesn't anyone ever write an ode to a basketball? A basketball that's been bounced around in the pro leagues would have some stories to tell, no doubt about it."

"This is absurd," Calico said.

Pierce turned toward her. "Socrates was fantastic. Didn't you get the message? Man is caught up in the need for materialistic things. Rather than accepting himself and others simply for who they are, he judges them by what they have."

"Well, amen to that," Abby said, looking pointedly at Calico.

"A grapefruit said all that?" Calico asked.

"Yep." Pierce smiled, appearing extremely pleased with himself. "The Blue Banana is a great place. I just wish I had known about it before tonight. If it hadn't been for Abby calling me and telling me to come here, I—"

"Uh-oh," Abby said.

"I knew it, I knew it!" Calico exclaimed. "This was a con, a scam." She jumped to her feet. "Abby, I hope you and Sticks live happily ever after and have forty-two children. I" —she lifted her chin—"am going home to Homer." She turned and started away, wiggling around the many tables and chairs between her and the door.

"Hey," Pierce called. "Calico?"

"Go after her, Pierce," Abby said.

"And do what? Say what?"

"Wing it. Calico is furious. I know Calico. She will forgive me for my part in this, but you're in a heap of trouble. Go."

Pierce stood. "I've never done anything like this before. I don't know what to say or . . . Oh, hell." He strode away.

Abby dropped her head into her hands. "What have I done?"

"Made me realize what an idiot I've been," Sticks said, awkwardly patting her shoulder. "I never dreamed I had a chance with someone like you, Abby. I used to daydream about it. You know, the two of us, together, and . . ."

"Oh, Sticks." She sighed wistfully, then raised her head. "Would you answer one question for me?"

"Anything."

"What's your real name?"

"Melvin."

"I'll call you Sticks."

"Good idea."

Outside, Pierce looked around frantically, then spotted Calico just as she was turning the corner. He sprinted down the sidewalk and caught up with her, then fell in step beside her without speaking. Several long, silent minutes passed.

"You're really ticked off," Pierce finally said.

"Really."

"I don't blame you, I guess. It was a pretty juvenile plan, but desperate people do desperate things. You walked out of that café with every intention of walking out of my life as well. I just couldn't let that happen, Calico. Can't you see that?"

"Pierce, please . . ."

"Look, I know you have goals, and you've

worked very hard to achieve them. Abby told me about your being raised by your grandmother, and that now you're on your own. I respect you for what you've done. I wouldn't do anything to keep you from accomplishing what you've set out to do. All I'm asking, Calico, is that you make a little space, a little time, for us."

"No."

He moved in front of her, forcing her to stop. The star-studded sky cast a silvery glow over them. He framed her face in his hands, and she met his gaze with a frown.

"You should listen to the grapefruit," he said quietly. "The grapefruit knows that it doesn't matter what we own. It's people themselves, who they are inside, their values, integrity, honesty, that count. Calico, please, give us a chance. Let's find the answers to the questions we have."

"No, I—"

"Questions, Calico Smith. Such as what it would be like to kiss you"—he lowered his head toward hers—"in the moonlight, under the stars." He flicked his tongue over her lips, and she shivered. "Such as what you'd taste like, how soft your lips would be. Questions. So many, many questions."

He dropped his hands from her face, gathered her close to his body, and captured her mouth with his.

Six

The kiss was, a happening.

The kiss was, for Calico, the most incredible experience she'd ever had.

She encircled Pierce's neck with her arms, her fingers inching into his hair, and returned the passionate kiss with total enthusiasm. She filled her senses to overflowing with the taste of him, the aroma, the feel of his thick hair, and of his strong, taut body.

A section of her hazy mind told her that the kiss was dangerous and should be ended at that very moment. But her heart spoke, too, with a far greater force, and she listened.

Savor, her heart whispered. Cherish. This was stolen ecstasy. She was being kissed by the most magnificent man she'd ever met, and was kissing him back with a sensuality she hadn't known she possessed. They stood in a glorious waterfall of silvery starlight that allowed nothing to intrude.

Oh, Pierce, Calico cried out silently. He'd ignited a wild passion within her, a swirling passion that threatened to consume her. Her breasts were crushed to the hard wall of his chest with a pain so sweet, it could only be described as exquisite.

Pierce released her mouth so he could trail enticing kisses across her cheek and down her neck. The answer to his question, he thought foggily, of what it would be like to kiss Calico Smith was beyond his imagination. It was an explosion of heated sensations, of want and need far greater than his wildest fantasies had envisioned.

This delicate creature in his arms was the epitome of womanhood, and she cast into oblivion the bevy of women in his past. There were no yesterdays, there was only now and the future. A future with Calico.

Oh, yes, Pierce thought, this was a happening, an experience, and he now knew that he didn't want it to end. Calico had changed his life irrevocably from the moment she'd appeared at his door as a human-size chicken.

He raised his head, but did not release his hold on her. She nestled against him as he rested his chin lightly on the top of her head. They both willed their overheated bodies to cool, their heartbeats to slow, their rough breathing to soften.

They stood quietly in the silvery cascade of light, and cherished the memories they'd just made, which were theirs to keep for all time.

Reality returned, and Pierce smiled.

Reality returned, and Calico sighed, her euphoria nudged aside by the heavy weight of sadness.

"That," Pierce said, his voice hoarse with passion, "was quite an answer to the question of what it would be like to kiss you. It's incredible."

"Pierce—"

Instinctively knowing he didn't want to hear what she had to say, he gripped her upper arms and gently moved her away from him. His smile was met by her troubled frown.

"We're headed in the wrong direction from where I parked my car," he said. "Would you like to get something to eat before we go back to Scottsdale?"

"No. No, thank you. I can catch a bus two blocks up from here."

"Don't be silly. You belong with me. I'll see you safely to Mrs. Weatherby's apartment." He cradled her face in his hands and stroked his thumbs over the soft skin of her flushed cheeks. "Kissing you was heaven, Calico," he whispered. "I'm sure you're aware of how much I want you, want to make love with you. You want me too. The way you kissed me delivered that message loud and clear."

"I—"

"No, wait, let me finish. I think it's important that you know I won't rush you or put any pressure on you. We'll make love when the time is right for both of us. Calico, you look so upset, but you shouldn't. Everything is fine, fantastic.

I'm a part of your life now, but I swear I won't do anything to stand in your way. You'll graduate in a couple of weeks and take the CPA test, just as you planned. There's nothing to worry about. Nothing."

"Oh, Pierce, you don't understand. My goals and obligations don't end in a few weeks. I have to find a job, I have loans to repay, I—"

"Hey, slow down. You've been on your own for so long, you're not accustomed to having someone help you carry the load. You're not alone anymore, Calico. It's you and me together, now. You can't deny that something very special is happening between us."

He dropped his hands from her face and slid one arm across her shoulders. "About-face, soldier. My car is three blocks away on the other side of The Blue Banana." He sneezed, then sneezed twice more in rapid succession. "Oh, Lord, there go my allergies. It's the oleander bushes all along the edge of this sidewalk. Come on, let's get away from here."

Calico opened her mouth to protest, but then shut it and mentally threw up her hands in defeat. She walked along the sidewalk with Pierce, held close to his body by his arm that still encircled her shoulders. She half-listened as he chatted cheerfully about his annoying allergy to flowers, while a jumbled mass of thoughts tormented her mind.

She was terribly confused, and very frightened. She felt as though she were slipping down a steep mountain, unable to control her flight or its speed. She was being whisked along to a place where she knew she didn't belong, yet a part of her wanted, with a deep aching need, to go.

But she couldn't. It was the wrong time, and it would be the wrong time for more than a year, until she'd satisfied herself that she could stand on her own two feet, independent and under obligation to no one. She couldn't allow any man—even a man as wonderful as Pierce, whose kiss had ignited a fire she knew would not be easily quenched—to distract her from her most essential goals.

Knowing that, however, did not lessen the despair that swept through her, did not stem the chilling waves of loneliness. To make room in her life for Pierce now was dangerous. It would put all she'd worked so hard for at risk, and she could not, would not, allow that to happen.

And if all of that wasn't enough to cause an ache in her heart and a knot in her stomach, there was still the issue of them being from worlds that were as different as day and night.

Pierce sneezed again, abruptly jerking Calico from her dismal reverie.

"I forgot to bring an allergy pill," he said apologetically. "I'll take one as soon as we get home."

"Mrs. Weatherby's apartment," Calico said quietly, "isn't my home, Pierce. It's just a set of expensive rooms that I'm watching over as a temporary job. My home is a small room in an old house, with a bathroom at the end of the hall that I share with three other people. When my Gran was alive, home was a tiny apartment with one bedroom. *You* are going home where you belong. *I'm* living out of a suitcase at Mrs. Weatherby's until she returns."

"Okay," he said, "if you want to get technical about it. Being at Mrs. Weatherby's is a temporary job, as you said, but living in a small room with the bathroom down the hall is temporary too. You're about to graduate from ASU, remember?"

She sighed. "Pierce, a whole new lifestyle isn't going to be handed to me with my diploma. I still have a long way to go to achieve my goals." She shook her head. "I know you believe you understand what I'm facing, what I have to do, but you can't, not really. You also don't understand that I have to do it alone. That's just the way it is. Facts are facts."

"You're wrong, but that's enough heavy talk for one night. How would you like some fat-free yogurt in a crisp oat bran cone? There's a place in Scottsdale that has them, and they're delicious."

"Thank you, but no. I'm very tired, Pierce. It's been a long, grueling week. I'm ready for a bubble bath, then bed."

"Oh. Well, sure. We'll go straight home. I mean, I'll see you to Mrs. Weatherby's door."

"Thank you."

During the drive from Tempe to Scottsdale, Calico stared out the side window of the car, not speaking. Pierce glanced at her often, his frown deepening with each passing mile.

Calico was shutting him out, he thought. She was sitting right there next to him, close enough to touch, yet he could actually feel the distance growing between them. He could visualize in his mind the protective wall she was building to hide behind, to protect herself from her own reactions to him.

He'd never been up against anything like this before, he realized. Whenever he was interested in a woman, he rarely had trouble convincing her to go out with him. If she did happen to say no, he was never deeply hurt, but simply looked for someone else.

Calico Smith, however, was a different page, chapter, a different entire book in his life. He even had a sneaky, and welcomed, suspicion that he was falling in love with his enchanting human-size chicken.

But, damn, he wondered, how did a guy woo and win a chicken who—oh, good Lord—a *woman* who was doing everything within her power to deny her growing feelings for *him*?

He didn't have the foggiest idea how to woo. But then again, how tough could it be? He'd accomplished everything he'd set out to do thus far in his life, hadn't he? Once he set his determined mind to it, the wooing and winning of one Miss Calico Smith would be a piece of cake.

Outside Mrs. Weatherby's apartment, Pierce unlocked the door with the key Calico had handed him, then pushed the door open and gave the key back to her.

"Sleep well," he said. "You really do look tired. There's a lot of that nasty flu I caught going around, so you should get plenty of rest as a preventive measure."

"I will," she said. "Well, I'll get as much sleep as I can. Next week I have final exams. I think I'm prepared, but I have plans to do hours of reviewing just to make sure. Then I'll restudy it all before the CPA exam in June. Busy, busy, that's what I'll be, all right." She attempted a smile, but failed miserably. "So . . . good night, Pierce. Thank you for the ride, and I'm glad you enjoyed the grapefruit at The Blue Banana and—"

He kissed her.

He pulled her into his arms, captured her mouth with his, and slipped his tongue between her lips, seeking and finding hers.

He kissed her, and she melted against him, wrapping her arms around his waist and leaning into his hard body.

He kissed her, and she kissed him, and desire soared as their hearts raced wildly.

But then he released her so suddenly, she staggered.

"Good night," he said, his voice gritty.

Calico opened her mouth, realized that nothing was going to come out, and snapped it shut. On trembling legs, she walked into the apartment, then closed the door behind her.

Pierce stood in the silent corridor for several long moments, staring at the closed door, then finally turned and walked slowly down the hall.

The battle was on, he thought, and he intended to win. Calico Smith would be his.

At exactly twelve noon the next day, Calico heard a light knock on her apartment door. She got up from the floor where she'd been sitting for several hours surrounded by books and papers.

"Oh, ow, oh," she said, as she realized her right foot had fallen asleep. She limped across the living room, then finally resorted to hopping as the knock was repeated. She opened the door to find a smiling Pierce Anderson standing there, holding a medium-size cardboard box.

"Hello," he said, and dropped a quick kiss on her lips. "Excuse me, ma'am." He sidled past her and strode toward the dining room.

Calico blinked, shook her head, then closed the door. She hobbled after Pierce, her sleepy foot now feeling like a zillion pins and needles were using it to practice a polka.

Pierce glanced back at her, then did a quick double take.

"What's wrong?" he asked. "Did you hurt your toe? Your foot? Your leg? Your body? Are you in pain? Why are you limping? Why didn't you phone me when you did whatever it is you did to yourself? What happened to cause you to walk with—"

"Cut!" she yelled, stopping and slicing one hand through the air. "My foot went to sleep and now it's waking up, that's all. I thought about calling the paramedics, but decided to bite the bullet and be brave." She paused. "Why are you here with that cardboard box?"

"Because I didn't have a wicker basket like they do in the movies."

She frowned. "Did that answer make sense?"

Pierce walked back to her and scooped her up into his arms.

"What on earth are you doing?" she exclaimed, her nose nearly pressed to his. Oh, mercy, she thought, there were those eyelashes, and those lips, and . . . "Well, Pierce?"

"Half-awake feet hurt like the dickens to walk on. So"—he started toward the dining table—"you won't walk on them."

He set her gently in a chair, patted her on the head, then proceeded to unpack the box. "Pardon me, madam," he said. He whipped out a linen napkin and placed it on her lap. "Close your mouth, Calico."

She dutifully closed her mouth, but continued staring at Pierce in complete amazement.

"Chicken salad for protein," he said as he lifted a small covered dish from the box. "Melba toast, low in fat content, high in fiber, in round and rectangular shapes," he went on, tapping another dish. "Fresh fruit, cut into bite-size pieces, vitamin C. This tall, skinny container is a special drink made up of milk, orange juice, and yogurt, whipped in the blender. Vitamins D, C, A, plus calcium. And, for dessert, one huge chocolate chip cookie. Sinfully sinful, but you deserve a reward for studying so hard."

She barely had time to blink before he leaned over, framed her face in his hands, and kissed her so thoroughly, so intensely, so deeply, that a whisper of pure sensual pleasure caught in her throat. Then, while her mind was still swirling in a deliciously hazy, passionate blur, he straightened, turned, and strode out of the apartment without a further word.

"Well," she said, rather breathlessly. "My goodness." Her gaze darted over the dishes spread out on the table, and a smile curved her tingling lips. "Oh, thank you, Pierce Anderson. Thank you so very, very much."

Back in his own living room, Pierce paced the floor, replaying over and over in his mind the scene that had just taken place.

The plan had gone great, he decided. He'd provided Calico with a well-balanced meal, shared with her a kiss that he had been desperately in need of, and exited stage left. The exit was very important. It showed her that he respected the fact that she didn't have time for him at the moment because she needed to study.

He stopped his pacing and frowned.

Calico didn't have time for him, he mentally repeated. Dammit, Calico didn't have time for him. No, now wait a minute. He had to remember to tack on the "at the moment." This second seat he was in was only temporary, and he'd be acting like a spoiled brat if he pitched a fit about it.

The problem was, he thought, dragging one hand through his hair, the way Calico talked, "temporary" was a tremendously long stretch of time. The path she was on included passing the CPA exam, finding a high-salaried job, and paying off her student loans.

If he was allowed to do nothing more than pop in and out of her life like a representative from Meals on Wheels, he'd end up having to wear a name tag so she'd remember who he was.

Well, hell, he thought, slouching onto the sofa, there went his good mood. The whole scenario was as depressing as a scheduled root canal. It could be months before Calico *really* had time for him, and he had no intention of waiting that long.

He stood up again and started for the kitchen. Protein. He needed protein. He always did his best thinking after a hefty dose of protein.

He sneezed and changed directions, heading for the bathroom.

First up, though, was an allergy pill. Oh, and a multiple vitamin. For the campaign that lay ahead, he had to be in tip-top form. His entire future was at stake here, because . . .

He stopped and squinted at the ceiling, reliving the kiss he'd just shared with Calico. He saw again her smiling face, heard the happy sound of her laughter, and vividly recalled the sweet taste and feel of her.

Oh, yes, he thought, she was something, his lovable, human-size chicken. Calico was lovable . . . and he loved her.

As quickly as that, he knew his love was etched in stone, carved into his heart as permanently as the initials he'd scratched on an old tree when he'd been about fourteen years old.

He was now and forever in love with Calico Smith.

Calico washed and dried the numerous little dishes that had contained her lunch, which she'd consumed to the last morsel. She placed the dishes carefully in the box, then set it on a chair by the door.

Sighing, she sat back down on the living room floor and lifted an open textbook onto her lap.

It had been a delicious meal, she mused. And Pierce had been so cute as he'd rattled off the nutritional value of each different item.

It had been more than a meal, she knew. It had been a thoughtful, caring gesture that had touched her heart, making her feel very special. And it had been a clear message from Pierce that he respected her need for time alone to study.

Alone, her mind echoed. Oh, darn, she was beginning to hate that word and all the stark images it evoked. She didn't want to be alone, not anymore, not since she'd met Pierce Anderson. She wanted him in her life, wanted to make love with him, become one with him, and . . .

  . . . and never let him go.

She pressed trembling hands to her suddenly flushed cheeks, shaking her head in a futile attempt to dispel the lifelike picture of Pierce that flitted enticingly before her eyes.

"No, no, no," she whispered. "He's not mine to have, not mine to love."

She forced herself to look at her textbook. But she couldn't read the words on the page because of the tears misting her eyes.

Seven

Since he was still contemplating his new line of attack to woo and win Miss Calico Smith, Pierce stuck with his original program through the remainder of the weekend.

He arrived at Mrs. Weatherby's door at mealtime, zoomed in, and deposited his food on the dining room table. The service included a complete explanation of the nutritional attributes of each selection, plus a long, toe-curling kiss, or two, or three, which rendered Calico breathless and rather dazed.

Sunday night, after washing, drying, and packing the little dishes in the box once again, she wandered around the large living room.

"Hi, Homer," she said as she passed the goldfish's bowl. "I just ate turkey-à la-something, wild rice, and a bunch of other healthy stuff. I've decided your life isn't boring, Homer, it's bliss. You have a very simple, uncomplicated existence, and I envy you that. Oh, Homer, what am I going to do?"

She flopped onto the sofa and stared up at the ceiling.

Before meeting Pierce Anderson, she mused, the question of "What am I going to do?" would not have been bouncing around in her brain. She'd known, for as long as she could remember, exactly what she was going to do.

During the entire weekend, while the majority of her mental energies were centered on studying, a tiny section of her mind was acutely aware of exactly what time it was, of how long it would be before Pierce would reappear at the door. Time shuffled along like a lazy soldier, minute by agonizing minute. And then, there he would be, making her heart race, her smile bright, and causing an aching desire to pulse deep within her. Looking so gorgeous and bringing his eyelashes with him, there he would be . . . Pierce.

When he left, he seemed to take the warmth from the room and the breath from her body. The second the door closed after him, she missed him, longed for him.

A part of her, she realized, wasn't quite complete when Pierce Anderson wasn't with her.

"Ohhh," Calico moaned. If she was falling in love with that man, she'd be so angry, she'd never speak to him again. It was the wrong time, he was the wrong man, and she'd wring his neck if he'd stolen her heart. She'd demand that he give her heart back and—

"And then they'd tote me off to the funny farm," she muttered.

Sighing wearily, she left the comfort of the soft sofa and returned to the dining table, which was strewn with papers and textbooks.

Study, Calico, she ordered herself. She'd study, study, study, and later when she slept, the gremlins might reward her with a luscious, tantalizing dream starring Pierce Anderson.

In the middle of Monday morning, Pierce walked slowly from his office toward the front area where Miriam had her desk.

Calico had not been at Mrs. Weatherby's earlier when he'd gone to deliver breakfast. That was understandable. Disappointing, but understandable. He could remember the bizarre final exam schedules from his own ASU days. It had seemed as though part of qualifying to graduate was determined by whether or not a person could figure out where and when he was supposed to take which test.

Pierce entered the reception area to find Miriam talking to Michael, the young, bespectacled architect Pierce had hired a year ago when the work load had become too much for one man.

"Hi, Pierce," Michael said, beaming. "Guess what? I'm going to be a father. Me. A father. Can you believe that? Lord, I'm flying high. A baby. Sara Sue is going to have our baby. Lord, look at the time. I'll be late for the appointment to present these plans." He snatched up a thick roll of blueprints from Miriam's desk. "I'm outta here. A baby, Pierce. Can you believe that?" He ran out the door.

Pierce stared at the door, then sank into the chair opposite Miriam's desk.

"He can't have a baby, Miriam," he said.

"This ought to be good," she said. "Okay, I'll risk it. Why not?"

"Well, because he's just a kid himself. I don't pay him enough to support a family. So . . . I'll give him a raise. Yes, good, a raise. But, Lord, Miriam, he can't have a baby."

"Dear, Sara Sue is the one who's going to have it, if you want to get technical."

"For crying out loud, I realize that. You know what I mean, though."

"Actually," Miriam said, frowning, "I don't. Why, pray tell, can't Michael and Sara Sue have a baby?"

Pierce lunged to his feet. "Because I don't have one!" he yelled, thumping himself on the chest.

Miriam's eyes widened. "What?"

"What?" Pierce said at the same time. He sank back heavily into the chair. "Ohmigod, this has gone further than I thought. I realize I'm in love with her. That's fine, great. Well, not totally great, because she's hung up on the test and the loans, and I'm still working on a new campaign to get her to fit me into her life. More time, much more time for us. Right?"

"Of course," Miriam said loyally, though she was totally confused.

"But, holy smokes, Miriam," Pierce went on, "I'm all the way to babies. What should I do?"

"Pierce, dear, if you haven't figured out by now how to make babies, there isn't an awful lot I can say."

"Miriam, I'm in no mood for your weird sense of humor."

"Peace, my child," she said, holding up both hands. "Calm down."

"No."

"Hush. Now then, let me see if I have this straight. You're in love. Oh, that's so wonderful. Your mother will be thrilled. I assume you're in love with Calico of the chicken suit?"

Pierce reached inside his inner suit coat pocket and pulled out the now rather bedraggled yellow feather he'd retrieved from the floor on the first day he'd met Calico. He brushed one fingertip over the edges, attempting to straighten the bent feathers.

"Yes," he said quietly. "I'm in love with Calico Smith."

"Oh, honey," Miriam said, "why do you look so sad? Being in love is glorious . . . or it should be. Now, back up to the part about tests and loans, or whatever it was you said."

"And grapefruit. I know she didn't get the message from the grapefruit at The Blue Banana, so there's that problem too. Social status, money, those types of issues."

"The grapefruit at the blue banana," Miriam repeated slowly. "You're flipping your switch again, Pierce."

"The Blue Banana is a coffeehouse in Tempe."

"I knew that," she said, smacking the desk with one hand. "Doesn't everyone?"

"Do you want to hear this or not?"

"Yes, yes, I'm listening."

"Well, see, Calico was raised by her grandmother because Calico's parents were killed in a car accident when Calico was a baby. Her grandmother passed on a couple of years ago, and Calico is alone. She's determined to be a CPA and . . ."

Miriam's gaze remained riveted on Pierce's face as he told her the entire story. When the telephone rang, she switched on the answering machine and urged him to continue.

"And that's it," he finally said, throwing up his hands. "Calico is fighting her feelings for me because she's afraid she'll be pulled off course and won't accomplish her goals. I could be patient for a while, Miriam, but Calico is talking about getting a job and paying back her student loans all on her own. Then to frost this lousy cake, she says we're from different worlds, poles apart on a social scale. What a mess. She's telling herself to keep away from me, and I'm all the way up to having a baby with her. Dammit, that woman is driving me crazy."

"My goodness," Miriam said, shaking her head, "what a complicated situation. I must say that I admire Calico for being so independent, so determined to follow through with her plans."

"Thanks a bunch," Pierce said, glaring at her.

"I'm not finished speaking, Pierce. Heavenly

days, brilliant motherly speeches aren't that short. We produce whole sermons at the drop of a hat. Pay attention."

"Okay, okay."

She folded her hands on the top of her desk. "Compromise is called for here, dear. Calico needs to see that she can allow herself to live beyond the confines of the rigid path she's set for herself. You, sir, for once in your life, must understand that you're not going to have what you want right this minute, simply because you've decided that's how it should be."

He stiffened in his chair. "I resent that. You make it sound as though I've just sat back and waited for everything to be handed to me. That's not true. I've worked extremely hard to establish Anderson Architects."

"I know that. I was here from day one, remember? But I've also known *you* from day one of your life. Your mother and I have been friends since the ice age. Land's sake, Pierce, you didn't even take stumbling, tentative steps when you first walked. At eleven months old, you just took off across the room and that was that. All through your growing years you—pardon the misquote—came, saw, and conquered whatever you set your mind on. Yes, you've worked hard, but that is a bit subjective. Compare your road to success to the road Calico is traveling."

He shook his head. "You weren't kidding about the sermon, Miriam. I realize that Calico has had a rough time of it. Lord, she even did a stint as a human-size chicken to earn money.

But, hell, I'm in her life now. I have the resources to pay off her student loans and provide her with a nice home. She could even choose how many hours a week she wanted to work as a CPA, and how much time she'd have for being a wife and mother. Dammit, Miriam, if she'd quit fighting her feelings for me, we could have it all . . . right now."

"Pierce, she has a mind, a brain. You can't program her like a robot, so that she'll perform the way you want her to."

"But—"

"No. You'd better keep that new word in your vocabulary . . . patience. I'm hard pressed to remember a time you've had to use it to any degree. Even when you were thrown for a loop by your allergies, you bounced back by reading stacks of books on health and putting into practice"—she smiled with loving exasperation—"*everything* you read. You took charge and were once again in control. But this time? Patience, my dear Pierce."

"Well, hell," he said, getting to his feet. He carefully replaced the yellow feather in his pocket, then looked at Miriam again. "I'm not getting any younger, you know. The big three-oh is right around the corner. I'm due, even overdue, for a wife, a family, a settled lifestyle, and a charted future. I didn't set out to fall in love with Calico, but I *am* in love with Calico, and I need—"

"Patience, patience, patience."

"Your record is stuck, Miriam," he muttered, and strode back down the hall.

"Oh, dear," Miriam said, shaking her head. "Oh, dear, dear."

At six-thirty that evening, Pierce knocked on Mrs. Weatherby's door. He was determined to convince Calico to go out for dinner, to take a break from what he assumed was another scheduled set of hours of concentrated studying. He could at least talk to her for an hour or so, instead of just depositing his offering of food and disappearing.

He knocked again, then his eyes widened when the door was finally opened.

"Why, hello, Pierce," an older woman said in surprise.

"Mrs. Weatherby," he said. "You can't be here. What I mean is, I was expecting Calico to . . . She didn't tell me you were due back today."

"I wasn't due back," Mrs. Weatherby said, and sighed. "I was seasick and miserable from the moment I stepped foot on that cruise ship. We finally put into a port where I could make flight connections to come home. The way I feel, I'd probably become ill taking a bath."

"I see," Pierce said. "I'm sorry you didn't have a good time."

"Live and learn. Anyway, Calico isn't here, which is obvious. She's such a sweet girl. She named my goldfish Homer. Isn't that darling? I don't mean to be rude, Pierce, but I think I'd best go lie down."

"Yes, of course. I apologize for disturbing you."

"That's all right. After a few days on solid ground, I'll be fine. Good night." She closed the door.

"Damn," Pierce muttered, then started back to his own apartment. He stopped suddenly. He didn't know where Calico lived. He had no idea where she was. Mrs. Weatherby had contacted her somehow, but he couldn't go pounding on a seasick woman's door again. "Well, dammit, I've lost my chicken!"

At nine o'clock that night, a none-too-happy Pierce Anderson stood on the porch of an old, in-need-of-paint two-story house that was located in a run-down neighborhood several blocks from the ASU campus.

He now qualified, he thought sullenly, for a private detective license. He'd tracked Calico down, but the task had not been easy.

Due to it being exam week, the establishments frequented by roaming students were nearly empty. He'd tromped from one place to the next, but none of the handful of people he'd encountered knew Calico.

Finally, he'd gone to the gym, where he'd spoken to a huge creature named Hoop Henderson. Hoop made Sticks seem like a midget. Sure, he knew Calico, Hoop had said, but it had taken Pierce twenty more minutes to convince the giant to divulge her address.

Now, here he was, sleuth extraordinaire, having at last arrived at the residence of the elusive Miss Smith.

And what a dump, he thought. How the dilapidated house remained standing during the wild wind- and rainstorms of the summer monsoon seasons, he'd never know. What paint was left on the wooden siding was peeling and cracked, the porch sagged beneath his feet, the screen door in front of him was hanging crookedly by one rusted hinge.

He opened the screen door with a great deal of caution, fully expecting it to come off in his hand, then stepped inside the house.

The aroma of lemon polish reached him immediately, and after he sneezed three times, he realized that everything within his view was immaculately clean. And extremely shabby. The tile in the entryway was cracked and chipped, the furniture in the living room to the left was faded and threadbare, as was the fringed area rug on the floor.

To his right was a narrow staircase, the steps exhibiting a few dabs of paint. He started up them, then hesitated as the wood creaked ominously under his weight. The banister wobbled when he gripped it, and he snatched his hand away as though he'd touched something hot.

As he cautiously made his way upward, he could hear the muted sound of music as well as a hum of voices and an occasional burst of laughter. The higher he climbed, the higher his temper rose.

At the top of the stairs he stopped in the small landing area and looked around, a deep frown knitting his brows. There was a closed door directly in front of him and a narrow hallway to the left. He could see a bathroom at the end of the corridor and two opened doors along the hall. He walked forward and peered inside the first room.

Calico was sitting on a narrow bed, her back propped with pillows against a once-white wall. A textbook and papers were resting against her drawn-up knees.

A small wooden dresser stood next to the bed, and a pale pink scatter rug lay on the floor. A faded, overstuffed easy chair held Abby Kolb, and on the floor, his long back braced against the chair, was Sticks. Soft music came from a plastic radio on the dresser.

The trio was engrossed in studying, allowing Pierce a moment to stand unobserved in the doorway.

Dammit, he fumed, Calico didn't belong there. So, okay, the house was clean, there was no graffiti on the walls, no roaches in the corners, no winos sleeping in the halls, but still . . .

Yet this was where Calico would remain if she followed through with her plan to graduate, pass the CPA exam, get a job, and pay back her student loans. For heaven only knew how long he'd be bringing her back to this place after taking her to the finest restaurants and theaters in town.

No. No way. Not a chance.

Calico Smith was the woman he loved, the only woman he had ever and would ever love. She didn't have to live this way, not anymore. She was his, and he could offer her not only his love for all time, but creature comforts she deserved to have as well. This place, this lifestyle, was absurd, and not meant for her. Enough was enough.

"Hello," he said.

Three heads snapped up, and three sets of eyes widened as they stared at him.

"Pierce," Calico finally said. She scrambled off the bed and came to where he stood in the doorway. "My goodness, you startled me. How did you know where to find me?"

"It wasn't easy," he said, no trace of a smile on his face. "Were you hoping I wouldn't be able to track you down?"

"Oh, no, of course not. Mrs. Weatherby came back so unexpectedly and . . . I was going to call you tomorrow after my exam. I had so much to review tonight that I thought it best to wait."

"I see. Well, I'd like to talk to you if you could take a break."

"You bet," Abby said, getting to her feet. "Unfold your body, Sticks. We'll go to my room."

Sticks rolled to his feet in one smooth motion.

"We'll be right next door if you need us, Calico," he said, looking at Pierce.

"She won't need us," Abby said. "Go, go, Sticks."

Pierce stepped into the room to allow the pair

to leave, then redirected his attention to Calico.

"May I shut the door?" he asked.

She nodded.

He closed the door, then his gaze swept over the room.

"It's not much, but it's home," Calico said, attempting a breezy tone of voice and failing. "Would you . . . would you like to sit down?"

"No."

"I would." She returned to the bed and sat on its edge, silently thanking her trembling legs for getting her there.

How strange, she thought, as she stared up at Pierce. Sticks was much bigger than Pierce, but Pierce somehow seemed to fill the room, forcing her attention to focus directly on him. He was so beautiful, so male, so . . . there. But *why* was he there?

"What did you want to talk to me about, Pierce?"

He cleared his throat. "Calico," he said, rather stiffly, "I love you."

She blinked. "Pardon me?"

"I said, I love you." His frown deepened. "I, Pierce Anderson, am in love with you, Calico Smith."

"You're in . . . Oh, you are not. People who are declaring their love don't look mad enough to spit nails. You don't love me." Or did he? she wondered. Oh, dear heaven, did he? "You're not even leering with lust, let alone gazing at me with loving desire. You're glaring as though I took your private parking space."

"It's difficult to do this with a romantic flair, Calico," he said, his voice rising, "considering that you disappeared without a word, then I finally found you in this—this place."

"Keep your voice down. The walls are very thin."

"The whole house is very thin. It'll probably collapse in the next big windstorm, or just get picked up and hurled away."

"Then I guess we won't be in Kansas anymore, Toto." She smiled. He glowered. "Sorry," she said swiftly. "Not funny. Pierce, this isn't an elegant house, but it's clean, and the landlady is a dear old soul. I tried to explain that we come from different social levels, but you wouldn't listen. So now you're here and can see for yourself. It's not great, but it's my home, and I won't have you insulting it."

"I didn't insult it, exactly. I just said this house is . . . thin. Forget that for now. Calico, I also said that I love you."

"Don't you dare love me, Pierce Anderson," she said, jumping to her feet. "I won't stand for it, do you hear me? I know how these things work. Well, not from experience, but I go to movies, I've had friends tell me, I read romantic novels. You're not talking to a complete dunce here. A medium dunce, maybe, but—"

"Calico—"

"No," she rushed on. "I will *not* tolerate your declaring your love for me, because the next thing you'll say is, 'How do you feel about me, Calico? Do you care for, love me, even a little bit?' You're not going to do that, Pierce Anderson, because then I'd have to get in touch with myself to find the answers, and I'd probably discover that I love you with every breath in my body, and I don't *want* to love you, so go away and leave me alone, because I'm studying the income tax legalities involved in a corporation declaring Chapter Eleven bankruptcy, and . . .'' She stopped and drew in a deep breath as she ran out of air.

"How do you feel about me, Calico?" Pierce asked, his voice low, rumbly, and very, very male. He took a step toward her. She moved back an inch or so. "Do you care for me?" He walked closer still. She retreated. "Do you love me? Even a little bit? Tell me. Tell me the truth, Calico Smith."

"I . . ." she started as she stepped backward again. She bumped into the bed and lost her balance, flopping onto the sagging mattress like a rag doll.

Pierce closed the remaining distance between them. He shifted her legs up onto the bed, swept the papers and books to the floor, and lay on top of her, catching his weight on his forearms.

"You were saying?" he murmured, his lips mere inches from hers. He gazed directly into her eyes, acutely aware of his aching arousal, which had been instantaneous, the moment his body had come in contact with hers. "What were you going to say?"

She had no idea, Calico thought foggily. Oh, he felt so wonderful, and smelled so good, and her bones were melting from the glorious sensations churning within her. He was gazing into her eyes, and he would not see her leering with lust at him. Oh, no. He'd find desire there, real and stark and raw, answering his questions with words she refused to speak aloud.

She loved him. Oh, dear heaven, how she loved him.

And if he didn't kiss her in the next three seconds, she was going to die from the sheer need to feel his lips, his tongue, meet hers. She had to taste him, savor him, drink of the very essence of him.

"Oh, Pierce," she whispered.

Her arms floated up to encircle his neck, her fingers inching into his thick hair. Her lips parted in a sweet invitation . . . and he kissed her.

The kiss was deep, hungry, searing. The tiny room, the lumpy mattress, the thin house disappeared. They weren't in Kansas anymore, nor in Tempe, Arizona. They were in a misty, rosy place, where no one existed but the two of them. Nothing existed but the wondrous kiss and the rampaging desire that consumed them.

Pierce broke the kiss to draw a raspy breath. "Tell me," he said, his voice rough. "Say the words. Oh, Lord, Calico, I need to hear you say the words."

No! her mind yelled. She mustn't say aloud what her heart could no longer deny. Those words held the power to crush her protective wall and leave her vulnerable, to pull her away from her goals. No, no, no.

"I love you, Pierce," she heard her soft voice say.

"Oh, thank God," he said, and claimed her mouth once more.

The kiss flung into oblivion the last, lingering thread of rational thought, of reason and reality.

"I want you, Calico," he murmured. "I want to make love with you, here, right here, in your place, your thin house."

"Yes. Oh, yes." She clutched his shoulders. "Here, Pierce, in *my* world."

"*Our* world. Wherever we are together is *our* world, Calico."

"No, it's not. I—"

"Shh."

He kissed her again, then slowly, reluctantly, moved off her to stand by the bed. He glanced at the door, then crossed the room to flick the lock into place. As he returned to her, she rose to meet him.

Their eyes never leaving each other, they shed their clothes, their hands seeming to perform the task of their own volition. Quickly they stood naked before each other, offering all that they were as a woman and a man. Offering love.

Calico's gaze trailed over every inch of Pierce, and she marveled at his beauty, the magnificence of his body that boldly announced his desire for her. He was taut and tanned, muscles perfectly proportioned from one part of him to the next. His chest was covered in curls a shade darker than the thick, silken hair on his head. He was Pierce, and she loved him.

"You're so beautiful," she whispered in awe and wonder.

"Oh, no, Calico," he said, "it's you who are incredibly beautiful."

His heated gaze swept over her, lingering on her kiss-swollen lips; her small breasts that seemed to beckon to him to touch them with his hands, suckle them with his mouth; the gentle slope of her hips and the sweet curve of her thighs; the dark thatch that covered the sweet haven of her femininity.

"You're exquisite," he said, unable to control the rough, passion-laden timbre of his voice. "Oh, Calico, I'll try not to rush this. I'll try to give you all the time you need, but, dear Lord, I want you so much."

She smiled and lifted one hand to him. He grasped her hand and tugged gently, urging her near. She went, molding her softness to his hard length, relishing, memorizing, rejoicing.

They tumbled onto the narrow bed, not caring that it was so small. All they needed was room for the one entity they would become as their bodies meshed. There was only enough space between them for their hands to roam, caress, discover mysteries, and cherish the treasures found.

Again and again their lips joined, and they tasted the honeyed nectar of rising desire, as their hands never stilled and their passions soared.

"Oh, Pierce, please," Calico said, "I want you. I've never felt so . . . It's as though I'm on fire. Please, please, come to me."

He shifted over her and kissed her, unable to speak past the strange ache in his throat. Raising his head, he met her gaze, then slowly, his eyes never leaving hers, he entered her body. She welcomed him with the moist heat of her desire, and he groaned at the exquisite sensation.

"Yes," she said, with a soft sigh of pure feminine pleasure. "Oh, yes."

Deeper, deeper, he went, his muscles quivering from forced restraint and the ecstasy rocketing through his body with a sweet pain.

The rocking tempo began gently, yet it built swiftly as their bodies rose together in perfect synchronization, faster, harder, pounding, thundering in a wondrous cadence. The tension tightened within them, swirling coils spinning them toward a center they both sought.

One wildly racing heartbeat apart, they reached the vortex, rapture exploding within them. They gasped each other's name, clinging together as the world was swept away.

Pierce collapsed against her, spent. Never before, he knew, had he experienced lovemaking such as this. But never before had he loved. He had fought for Calico, and he had won. She was his, the future was theirs, and he was filled with the greatest joy he had ever known.

"I'm too heavy for you," he said finally.

"Oh, no, you feel wonderful. It was wonderful.

We were wonderful. I never knew it could be like that. I have very little to compare it to, Pierce, but I truly never dreamed that it . . ." She sighed happily.

He smiled. "I'm glad. We need to talk, Calico, make plans, but not right now." He carefully moved off her and nestled her close. "If we fall off this bed with a thud, everyone in this thin house will know it."

"I have a sneaky feeling," she whispered, "that Abby and Sticks aren't paying attention to anything beyond the two of them."

"Ain't love somethin'?" Pierce said, chuckling. "It's as contagious as that flu I had."

"Oh, nice comparison, Anderson." She yawned. "I feel heavenly, and sooo sleepy."

"Then close your gorgeous blue eyes."

"Mmm," she said, her lashes drifting down.

"We *will* talk, Calico, later. There's so much to discuss. But tonight is for us, and the beautiful memories we made that won't ever be forgotten. I love you, Calico Smith."

"I love . . . you, too, Pierce . . . Anderson," she murmured, then sleep claimed her.

Pierce held her protectively in his embrace, gazing down at her, then at last gave way to the somnolence that crept over him.

Eight

Calico opened her eyes, stretched, yawned, and knew without looking at the clock that it was six A.M. She'd perfected the knack years before of setting a subconscious mental alarm, and it had never failed her.

Five more minutes, she thought, still foggy with sleep. She'd give herself the luxury of not moving for five minutes, then she'd leap into action. No, actually, she'd crawl out of bed, mumbling and grumbling, as was her usual routine. While cheerful once fully awake, she was definitely not a rise-and-shine morning person.

As she drifted back into the deliciously hazy limbo of semi-asleep, she was vaguely aware that something was nagging her, prodding her to sweep away the cobwebs in her mind and become alert *right now*.

She frowned and forced herself to concentrate. In the next instant, her eyes flew wide open and she sat bolt upright.

Pierce.

The events of the previous night raced through her mind, like a movie set on fast-forward. Sweet desire swirled within her as she vividly relived the exquisite lovemaking she'd shared with Pierce.

Pierce . . . who had declared his love for her. Pierce . . . who had heard her declare her own love for him. Pierce . . . who had, indeed, stolen her heart, and who apparently didn't intend to give it back.

Suddenly realizing that she was naked as the day she was born, instead of wearing her Mickey Mouse nightshirt, she snatched the sheet and clutched it in tight fists beneath her chin.

But a thin sheet, she knew, was not going to take the place of the protective wall that had once surrounded her. Her defense against anything or anyone who might lure her from her goals was gone, smashed to smithereens by Pierce "Incredible Eyelashes" Anderson.

Oh, how she loved him, Calico thought dismally. And, oh, how she wished that she didn't. She felt so helpless, so vulnerable, so out of control. Falling in love for the first time should be joyful, wondrous.

Instead, she was terrified, and had the urge to cut and run as fast and as far as she could. Run back to the familiar path where she belonged.

What on earth was she going to do? she wondered. It was all so confusing, so muddled.

But at that moment, she had to center her attention on the exam she was taking that morning, an important test that needed her total concentration.

She left the bed and pulled on an enormous chenille robe that covered her from chin to toes. It was her trek-down-the-hall-to-the-bathroom robe that was faded and worn, but had seen her through her entire college years. She gathered clean clothes, then saw the note propped against the plastic radio on top of her dresser.

I love you, Calico, it read. *I'll see you tonight. Pierce.*

"Ohhh," she wailed, blinking back tears. "What a mess."

The day was long and very hot, and it was a weary Calico Smith who walked along the sidewalk toward her boardinghouse.

She'd done well on the exam, she knew. It would be several days before grades were posted, but from the moment she'd opened the folder and read the first question, she'd felt confident that she had the material down pat.

After the exam, she'd conducted back-to-back tutoring sessions, cleaned the living room—a very messy living room—of one of the fraternity houses, and walked and watered a professor's basset hound. And during all those hours, she'd thought of Pierce.

She was not one iota closer to having the answer to the nagging question of "What was she going to do?" and was exhausted from having that query echo over and over in her mind.

As she turned onto the walkway that led up to the house, she stumbled slightly in surprise at seeing Abby and Pierce sitting on the front steps.

"Yoo-hoo, Calico," Abby said, smiling. "How's this for a welcoming committee?"

"Very nice," Calico said, managing a small smile. She stopped in front of the pair, then slowly met Pierce's gaze. "Hello, Pierce."

He smiled at her, and she saw desire ignite in his eyes. Heat began to swirl and pulse deep within her.

She was only vaguely aware of Abby popping up, announcing that Sticks had just come into view at the end of the block, and dashing off to meet him.

Calico simply stood there, pinned in place by Pierce's mesmerizing gaze, hardly breathing as she relived yet again the wondrous lovemaking they had shared.

"Calico," Pierce asked, his voice low, "what's your favorite color?"

She blinked. "Pardon me?"

He held out one hand to her. "Sit down here by me. Okay?"

She sat on the step and looked questioningly at him. He brushed his lips over hers, and she instantly wanted more, much more.

"Things happened very quickly between us," he said, gazing directly into her eyes. "That's terrific as far as I'm concerned, but we sort of skipped over the getting-to-know-you-better chit-chat. So, therefore, what's your favorite color?"

"Blue."

"Blue is my favorite color too. Would you rather read or watch television?"

"Read. My favorite novel is the one I happen to be engrossed in at the time."

He nodded. "Interesting. I like that. Sports?"

"I don't play any, mostly because I don't have the time, but I love to watch Sticks on the court during basketball season. He's fantastic, absolutely awesome."

"Calico, how many . . . how many children would you like to have?"

"Oh, Pierce," she whispered, "don't."

"Don't what?" He framed her face in his big hands, and his gaze flickered over her features, lingering a long moment on her lips, before returning to her eyes. "Don't think about us, our future together, all the wonderful things waiting for us out there? Don't think about last night, our night, our unbelievably beautiful night? Don't love you with all my heart, soul, body, and mind? Oh, my lovely Calico, you ask the impossible."

No, she thought, panic rising swiftly within her, *he* was asking the impossible of *her*. She wanted—oh, how she wanted—a future with Pierce. To be his wife, his other half, the mother of his children; to grow old with him, stay by his side until death parted them. . . . It all painted a picture in her mind that was enticing, almost irresistible.

But how could she divide herself into so many sections? She couldn't—not and do justice to any of the multitude of roles she would be attempting to juggle. Not only would she be a CPA, have large debts to pay, but she would also be a wife in a social structure of which she knew little, a mother . . . No, she couldn't do it. She couldn't have it all.

Pierce Anderson was, indeed, asking the impossible of her. And that was just so incredibly sad.

Two tears slid down her cheeks.

"Oh, hey, what's this?" Pierce asked. He caught the tears with his thumbs. "You've had a helluva day, right? I remember the stress of exam week. It's hard on the system, especially since it falls at this time of year, when it's getting so hot and—*Achoo!* Excuse the sneeze. And any allergies you might have are driving you nuts. *Achoo!* Look, let's go to an air-conditioned restaurant and get something to eat."

"But—"

"You have to eat properly if you intend to do the best work possible on your exams. The correct level of protein, vitamins, all of that, is vitally important for you to achieve your maximum potential. Therefore, a steak, salad, vegetables, and a fruit cup for dessert are in order." He dropped a quick kiss on her lips, then stood. "Ready?"

"But . . ." Calico started, then sighed. "Yes, all right, Pierce, we'll go eat."

"Great. Do you want to put your tote bag in your room first?"

"No, I'll carry it. I'm so used to hauling it around, I'd probably feel as though a part of me was missing if I didn't have it. This beat-up old bag has been with me for a lot of years."

He frowned as he looked at the tote bag, then at her again.

"Yes," he said, slowly nodding, "I understand what you're saying."

She cocked her head, puzzled. "You have the strangest expression on your face," she said. "Do I have a bug on my nose?"

"No, I—*Achoo!* Oh, for Pete's sake, let's get out of here. I'm losing the allergy battle to the oleander bushes in this neighborhood."

His car was parked a block away, and they walked in silence, Pierce's arm around Calico's shoulders. She blanked her mind and refused to think, refused to listen to the warring voices in her head. She was so tired, and so confused, and had such a bad case of the blahs and the blues, she felt like a heavy stone had landed on her heart.

She'd concentrate, she decided wearily, on steak, salad, vegetables, a fruit cup for dessert, and for now, at least, the rest of her woes could take a flying leap.

As they drove to a casual family restaurant, she had the strange sensation that she was floating outside of herself, a passive observer of the couple in the expensive sports car.

She heard herself answering Pierce's questions regarding her hectic day, what exams were yet to come, the fact that graduation was only slightly more than a week away and that she didn't intend to take part in the official ceremony.

"Why not?" he asked as he led her into the restaurant. "Hold that thought. Here comes the hostess."

They were shown to a booth, a waitress instantly appeared, and Pierce ordered duplicate dinners of steak, salad, vegetables, and fruit cup for dessert.

Calico landed back in reality with a thud when he repeated his question as to why she wasn't going to take part in the graduation ceremony.

Well, drat, she thought. She'd rather liked it in her other-world place, where she could pick and choose what she did, or did not, wish to dwell on.

"I just don't have any reason to attend the ceremony," she said. "I'm interested in the certificate, not in wearing a cap and gown, and getting a tassel that I can hang on the mirror in my car. I don't own a car, and I don't have any family to watch me receive my diploma. So . . ." She shrugged.

"*I'd* be there," he said quietly.

"That's very nice of you, Pierce. Thank you, but it isn't necessary. I really don't want to go.

Abby agrees with me. She said she hates long-winded speeches. Her family lives in Chicago and can't afford to come out, anyway."

"Okay," he said, "so why don't you and I have our own celebration? You know, go out to dinner at a fancy place, toast your graduation with champagne, the works."

"A fancy restaurant?"

He smiled. "Five-star, state-of-the-art."

"I—I don't have anything to wear to a swanky place like that."

"I'll buy you a dress."

"No."

"Why not? It's traditional to receive gifts when you graduate. So, my gifts to you are a new outfit and a night on the town. There's nothing wrong with that. It sure beats the fourteen pen-and-pencil sets and twenty-two pairs of cuff links I got when I graduated. I don't even wear cuff links. Hey, treat me right, and I'll toss in a pen-and-pencil set as part of the deal."

She laughed. "You're so crazy." Her smile faded. "And so dear, and thoughtful, and I . . ." Her voice trailed off.

"Say it, Calico," he urged her. "Say, 'I love you, Pierce.'"

"Oh, I do love you, Pierce, but . . ."

"Halt. The word 'but' doesn't go on the end of that. Now then, we eat our protein and vitamin dinner, then we're off to the boutiques. We're going to find you a sensational dress."

"I was going to look over some material for tomorrow's exam and . . . Oh, for heaven's sake, I know the stuff for that class backwards and forwards."

"Good. Eat."

"But then again," she went on, "I'm not sure if I should accept something as personal as a dress from you."

He leaned toward her, a glint of amusement in his eyes.

"My darling Calico," he murmured, "you *accepted* something far more personal than a dress from me last night in your skinny little lumpy bed."

"Oh," she said, then shut her mouth as she felt a warm flush heat her cheeks.

As they were finishing their fruit cup dessert, Pierce took a small tin box from his pocket, popped it open, and removed one white pill and one orange pill. He swallowed them with the last of his milk.

"What were those pills for?" Calico asked.

"The orange was for my allergies. The white . . . See, my sinuses clog up when I come into an air-conditioned place after being out in the heat. I've often said there should be a city ordinance passed stating that every public building have a temperature-change area. It would save a great many people unnecessary problems with their sinuses."

Calico smiled at him with loving amusement. She'd never known anyone who was such a worrywart about every little aspect of his health. When it came to diet, pollution, pollen, vitamins, and everything else imaginable, Pierce was like a fussy old man. But when it came to making love? Now *that* was definitely a deliciously different story.

As they drove to a mall that Pierce said had a lot of fancy shops, Calico decided it just wasn't proper for him to buy her a dress. The subject had never come up during Gran's dos and don'ts teachings, because there hadn't been men forming a line to buy Calico dresses. Still, she told herself, this would never do.

She'd wiggle out of the situation gracefully. She'd examine the selection of dresses in a few stores, then sigh, shake her head, and simply state that there wasn't anything she liked. And that would be that. Goodness, her genius-level mind amazed her at times.

The boutique was called Rainbow's Walk. Calico's eyes widened and her breath caught when they entered the store.

The clothes had been arranged by color, rather than by the type of article. Each color began with the palest shade and moved gradually toward deep, vibrant hues.

"Oh, my," she said, and sighed wistfully. Her clever plan had vanished in a poof.

Pierce kissed her on the temple. "Shall we walk through this rainbow? Which color do you want to stop at along the way?"

"Blue," she whispered.

"Blue, it is," he said, taking her hand. "Come on."

The dress was the shade of a robin's egg. Made of an elegant-looking linen, it was tailored and slim-fitting, with short sleeves, an open neckline, and decorative buttons down the front. Though simply styled, it was distinctly feminine, and Calico felt like a modern-day Cinderella greeting her Prince Charming as she walked out of the fitting room for Pierce's inspection.

He rose slowly from the velvet-covered chair where he'd been sitting, his gaze sweeping over her. He could feel the wild cadence of his heart, and the heat that shot through his lower body.

"Lovely," the gray-haired saleswoman said.

"Lovely," he repeated, his eyes riveted on Calico.

"Absolutely perfect," the woman added.

"Perfect," he echoed, his voice sounding strange to his own ears.

"It's as though it was custom-made for her," the woman said.

"*She* was custom-made for *me*," he said.

Then he crossed the room, gathered Calico into his arms, and kissed her.

He raised his head only far enough to speak. "Let's go home."

"Yes," she said dreamily. "Oh, yes."

The blue dress was carefully folded within layers of pale blue tissue inside a glittering white box, and Calico placed the box on her lap when she settled onto the seat in Pierce's car.

He glanced over at her and chuckled. "It won't break."

"Oh, Pierce, it should be treated like a precious treasure. I have never in my life had a dress so beautiful, so . . . When I was wearing it, I felt . . . Oh, dear, I can't find the words. Thank you so much for this gift."

"You're welcome," he said, turning the key in the ignition. "You deserve a closet overflowing with beautiful clothes, Calico. In fact, that's exactly what you're going to have."

"Someday," she said, caressing the sparkling box. "Oh, not a closet overflowing, like you said, but a few pretty things, special things to wear to . . ." Her hand stilled, and she frowned. "The Blue Banana? Good grief, I don't have anywhere ritzy to go in my imaginary clothes."

"Dammit, Calico," Pierce said, smacking the steering wheel with the heel of one hand. "You're doing it again. You keep . . . I don't know . . . erasing me from your life, acting as though I am going to dissolve into thin air. We love each other, remember? I'm talking about forever and ever love, the until-death-parts-us kind of love."

"But I—"

"I want to marry you!" he yelled. Calico jumped, nearly knocking the box to the floor. "Did I mess this up," he asked, "—did I not get that across to you?" He shook his head, and his voice was gentle when he spoke again. "Yes, I blew it. I realize that now. I should have properly proposed to you, had a ring to give you in one of those fuzzy little blue boxes. Ah, damn, where was my brain? I'm sorry, I really am."

"Pierce—"

"Well, I'm not going to propose while I'm trying to keep from getting creamed in this traffic. I'm not saying another word until we get to my apartment. You keep quiet too. Okay? No more talking until we're safely in my living room together."

"But, Pierce—"

"Shh. There's a cement truck behind us with a driver who seems to be considering going right over the top of my car. I'm stressing out. I am most definitely stressing out."

Calico sighed, but did not say another word.

In Pierce's living room, Calico placed the dress box on a chair, then slowly, tentatively, withdrew her hands as though she'd just set down a fragile, decorated cake.

Pierce watched her, shaking his head. The women he knew took dresses like that one for granted, just stuck them in a closet next to the dozen or so others already there.

Calico's reaction to the blue dress was refreshing, adorable . . . and heartbreakingly sad. When they were married, he'd see to it that she had everything she'd been denied as she'd grown up.

She'd been deeply loved by her grandmother, he knew, and now *he* loved her, and it was Calico's turn for luxuries, for the removal of the pressure caused by debts and endless part-time jobs. He was there, and things were going to change.

"Calico," he said quietly.

"Yes?"

"I still don't have the little blue box with the ring in it, but I'll get it. Right now, though, I'm going to ask you, even without a ring to slip on your finger." He closed the distance between them and placed his hands on her shoulders. "Calico Smith, will you do me the honor of becoming my wife? Will you marry me? Please?"

She would not cry, Calico told herself. She would not burst into tears and weep all over the front of Pierce's shirt. And she would not pretend, for one moment longer, that she could stay in his world for the remainder of her days.

"Calico?"

"No," she whispered, hardly able to speak past the lump in her throat. "No, I can't marry you."

"Why not?" he asked, his voice gentle.

"You *know* why, Pierce. Ignoring facts won't make them go away. I'm not free to marry anyone. I have to finish what I've set out to do, including paying off my debts. It will be a long time before I can think about anything other than the goals that I *must* achieve. Please don't make this more difficult than it is. I love you, but I can't marry you."

"Come sit down."

"There's no point in discussing this further."

"Please, just sit on the sofa with me and listen to what I have to say."

She sighed. "All right, but . . ."

"Shh." He took one of her hands and led her to the sofa. She sat ramrod stiff, her hands folded tightly in her lap. He sat down close to her, shifting so that he was facing her. "Calico, would you look at me, please?"

"No."

"Do you want me to talk about something this important while I'm staring at the side of your head?"

"That's a great deal safer than my staring at your eyelashes."

"Would you ignore my eyelashes, for Pete's sake?"

She slowly turned her head to meet his gaze. "Your eyelashes are not ignorable."

He looked up at the ceiling and mentally counted to ten. In control again, he looked at her once more.

"Calico, I love you and you love me. That's the foundation of our relationship—love. When two people are building their lives together on a firm base of true love, there is nothing that can defeat them."

"That was beautiful," she whispered. "Did you read that somewhere?"

"No, I made it up," he said, nearly yelling. He took a deep breath and let it out slowly. "Easy, Anderson. Don't lose it. Calico, just listen, okay?"

"Yes."

"Good. Now then, I realize that you set goals for yourself long before I met you. I understand what those goals are, and I respect and admire you for having them."

"Thank you."

"Don't interrupt."

"Sorry."

"You'll accomplish your goal of graduating in the next week. You'll accomplish your goal of becoming a CPA when you pass the exam next month. You'll accomplish your goal of getting a job as soon as you present your credentials to a CEO, or whoever, who has even half a brain. I'd be the last person on earth to keep any of that from happening."

"That's comforting," she said, nodding. "Oh, sorry," she tacked on quickly when he glared at her. "Forget I spoke. Carry on."

"Thank you. That leaves your student loans. My wedding gift to you would be to pay off those loans. I'll write a check and—"

She jumped to her feet. "You certainly will not."

He tugged on her hand until she sat back down.

"Would you hear me out?" he said. "Cancel that plan. Try this. We get married, you work, and all your income goes toward paying off the student loans. I make enough to support us. I'll take care of you while—"

She leapt to her feet again. "You certainly will not."

"Your record is stuck. Sit down."

She plopped back onto the sofa and crossed her arms beneath her breasts.

"Pierce, those debts are mine," she said, staring straight ahead. "Both of your ideas are, in actuality, the same thing. Whether you write a check or support me while I pay off the loans, it still means I'm not taking care of my obligations in the manner that I have always intended to. I can't allow you to do that." She turned her head to look at him. "Can't you see that?"

"No. You're clinging to those debts just like you hang on to your tote bag."

"What?"

"Before we went to dinner, I asked you if you wanted to put your tote bag in your room so you wouldn't have to lug it around. Granted, the bag is, at the moment, still in my car because you carried the dress box up here, but the principle is there."

"What do you mean?"

"You said that your tote bag was a part of you, that you'd feel as though something was missing if you didn't have it with you. I'm no shrink, but I think you were understandably frightened when your grandmother died and you were left all alone. So, you cling to the familiar, getting a sense of security from following a set program, something that is well-known and you can control."

"Pierce . . ."

He raised one hand to silence her. "Falling in love with me threw you off course and scared you to death. You're on foreign ground again, and it's terrifying. So, you're frantically scrambling back to the familiar and holding on tight.

Your tote bag, the debts, your absurd stand on social status, have been with you for a long time. Your burdens are heavy, but you know exactly what they are. Moving forward with me is stepping into the unknown. Oh, Calico, am I making any sense at all?"

She shook her head. "I don't like what you're implying, Pierce. You're making me sound as though I'm hanging on to something as troublesome as owing a large amount of money as I would to an old teddy bear or baby blanket. Why not just stamp the word 'neurotic' on my forehead and be done with it?"

"I didn't say what I said to insult you, Calico. I'm fighting a tough battle here, with our entire future together at stake. I'm not saying my theory is right, either. All I'm asking is that you think about it, consider the validity of the concept."

"I'll do no such thing, Pierce Anderson, because it's absurd. I won't allow you to step in and pay my debts with either of your fancy plans because of my integrity, my self-esteem, the value I place on who I am as a person. That is a far cry from your analysis. In my opinion, your deductions are stinky and, yes, extremely insulting."

"Dammit, if you insist on being so stubborn about this, about doing it all yourself with no help, how are we going to have a chance at a future together? You could be years paying back those loans. Good Lord, Calico, are you going to throw away what we have together because of a goal you set before we even met? Love changes lives, but if you aren't willing to adjust, compromise, that love doesn't have a glimmer of hope of surviving. Your refusing to give even an inch means that our love doesn't have one iota of room to grow."

"My," she said sarcastically, "it must be marvelous to be such an expert about love."

"I don't know squat about love. What I'm saying is just plain, everyday common sense."

"Are you insinuating that I don't have any common sense?" she exclaimed.

"I'm saying that . . ." He stopped speaking, closed his eyes, and frowned, "I think I'm getting an ulcer." He pressed one hand on his stomach and opened his eyes. "Lord, I hope I'm not getting an ulcer, because I'd probably have to eat vanilla pudding, and I really hate vanilla pudding. Do you realize that we're arguing, Calico?"

"Well, yes, I guess we are. My stomach doesn't feel too terrific, either."

"Look, I think I jumped the gun here. You're in the middle of exam week, and that's enough stress for a person. Why don't we put this all on hold until after you've graduated?"

"Nothing is going to change by then, Pierce."

"You never know. My proposal of marriage stands as stated. As for your answer to that proposal and all this other stuff . . . it's taboo until after you have your diploma in your hand. Agreed?"

"Yes, but—"

"Shh. There's that word again." He inched

closer to her and slipped one arm around her shoulders. "That's enough war for tonight. It's time to make love." He lowered his head toward hers. "Love is much better for potential ulcers than war. Much, much better."

His mouth melted over hers, and she responded instantly, eagerly, hungrily. Desire burst free within her like leaping flames of a fire that consumed her.

She was playing mind games, she knew, pretending that if she didn't acknowledge the hopelessness of a future with Pierce, the dismal situation would simply disappear. She had been a fairly good human-size chicken, but obviously was excellent at impersonating an ostrich.

She didn't care, though, not now, because Pierce was holding her and Pierce was kissing her, and soon, very soon, he was going to make love to her.

And he did.

Nine

To Calico's amazement the following days fell into a pattern that was absolutely delightful. She had, she soon realized, actually managed to push her problems, her lingering blahs and blues, all thoughts beyond the moment that she was living, to a dusty corner of her mind.

The days were made up of studying for and then taking scheduled exams, as well as performing various agreed-upon odd jobs. The nights were centered on Pierce.

They ate at whatever casual restaurant met their fancy, with Pierce scrutinizing the menu before ordering, to insure that they were meeting the daily requirements from the four basic food groups.

One night they went to a special showing of *Casablanca*, which made Calico cry so much at the ending, she got the hiccups. While they ate frozen yogurt afterward, Pierce listened attentively—despite bursting into laughter several times—as Calico verbally rewrote the last scene of the movie, giving it an "and they lived happily ever after" ending.

Another night they sat on a blanket on the grass on the ASU campus and listened to a band that played swing music from the thirties and forties.

On Saturday, they drove to Encanto Park for a canoe ride. The enormous park was bursting with vibrant summer flowers, and Pierce sneezed his way across the lake. Calico was convinced that one more hefty "achoo" was going to spill them into the water, and held on to the edges of the canoe with her eyes tightly closed.

Abby and Sticks joined them on Sunday for pizza, and everyone good-naturedly ate the oranges Pierce produced for dessert.

The four then played gin rummy for hours at Pierce's apartment, using no fat, no cholesterol oatmeal cookies to bet with. Sticks won the biggest pot, then gave the cookies to Abby, announcing that he wasn't into eating sawdust.

Oh, and the nights, Calico often mused dreamily. They were glorious, lovemaking nights with Pierce. They were ecstasy. Passion flared at the slightest touch or smoldering gaze between them, and they reached for each other eagerly, anticipating the wondrous meshing of their bodies into one entity.

They declared their love aloud whenever the

mood struck, not caring where they were or who might hear.

Calico savored every sunshine-filled day and lovemaking-filled night, every hour, every minute, treating each as a cherished gift and precious memory. There was no future beyond the next beat of her heart—a heart that seemed to be bursting with love for Pierce Anderson.

Friday evening, Calico sat on the edge of her bed wearing only a slip. It was graduation night.

She'd filled out the necessary form requesting that her diploma be mailed to her, and was now preparing for her night of celebration with Pierce. The beautiful blue dress was carefully laid out next to her on the bed.

Well, she thought, she'd done it. She'd obtained a bachelor's degree in accounting from Arizona State University. So where was the elation, the hip-hip-hooray euphoria, that should have her giddy with relief, excitement, and a tremendous sense of accomplishment?

She didn't know where they were, but she certainly wasn't feeling ecstatic. How strange, she mused. After working so hard for so long, she'd fully expected to be practically bouncing off the walls at graduation time.

So, why wasn't she? She was looking forward to her splendid evening ahead with Pierce, yet this planned dinner seemed completely separate from this day, which marked the end of a long, tedious struggle that had culminated in her reaching part of her goal.

She stiffened, her eyes widening as she silently repeated that last thought. She had reached *part* of her goal. *Part.* Because her ultimate goals were so enormous, encompassing so many steps, she had robbed herself of the bliss connected with something as momentous as graduating from a major university.

"Well, drat," she said aloud.

The revelation was disturbing, and definitely not what she wanted. Anyone, no matter what he or she had yet to accomplish, should lift his glass high in a toast to himself for earning a college degree.

She pressed her fingertips to her temples in an attempt to halt the tumbling mass of confusion in her mind. Her reaction, or rather the lack of it, to having a bachelor's degree was going to be shoved into that corner of her brain for now. She could only hope there was room for one more dilemma that she was refusing to face until later.

Yes, *later*, she told herself, because tonight was Pierce, and the beautiful blue dress, silvery stars twinkling in the heavens like millions of diamonds, smiles, and laughter, and love.

Tomorrow she would return to reality. Tomorrow could very well be the first of a multitude of lonely days and nights. Tomorrow she would probably cry.

"But not tonight," she said, getting to her feet. She lifted the dress from the bed. "Oh, no, not tonight." She smiled. "Tonight is magic and memories. Tonight is Pierce."

• • •

Pierce ate his dinner by rote, unable to keep his attention on anything other than Calico. Her eyes were dancing with excitement, sparkling like priceless sapphires, as her gaze swept over the plush dining room of the restaurant time and again.

"Oh, Pierce," she said, "it's like something out of a movie. I can't believe I'm really here. Look at those chandeliers. Have you ever seen anything so splendid? And this china. It's so delicate, and with gold edging. Can you imagine?" She laughed. "Is the food good? I can't remember a thing of what I've eaten."

"I'm certain the food is first-rate," he said, smiling, "but I wouldn't know. I've been too engrossed in watching you." His smile faded. "You're so good for me, Calico. You make me see things through your eyes, things I've taken for granted for a long time. If it weren't for you, I wouldn't be able to say later what this room looked like. It *is* beautiful, and I'm appreciating that. And *you* are beautiful, and I'm most definitely appreciating that."

"Thank you," she said, "but do give proper credit to the dress too. It's so lovely." Her gaze flickered over him, noting his custom-tailored dark blue suit, light blue shirt, and blue-toned paisley tie. Oh, the man was devastating. "Your shirt is nearly the exact shade of my dress."

"Not by accident, my love. I wasn't going to do or say anything tonight to 'clash' with you. This is your special evening, Calico, and I want it to be absolutely perfect."

Before she could reply, a couple in their late forties appeared beside their table. They were extremely attractive and, Calico decided, the diamond ring on the woman's finger probably cost six times more than Hoop Henderson's so-called car.

"Hello, Pierce," the woman said. "How very nice to see you."

Pierce stood up and introduced the pair to Calico as Betsy and Jack Brooks.

"Now, Jack," Betsy said to her husband, as Pierce sat back down, "don't you dare suggest that we join Calico and Pierce for a bit. These young people are obviously out on the town for a special occasion."

"Well, damn," Jack said, smiling. "Cut off at the pass. I wanted to discuss my idea for the pool area with Pierce. I've decided to add an old-fashioned gazebo, Pierce. What do you think? Calico, this young man is one of the finest architects I've ever had the pleasure of working with. He designed our new home in Paradise Valley."

"Oh," Calico said, nodding. Now what did she say? she wondered frantically. How big is your house? No, that was crass. Oh, good grief, these people were obviously wealthy, and there she sat, not having the foggiest idea how to talk with them. "I'm sure you have a lovely home," she said lamely.

"We'll get together next week, Jack," Pierce

said. "I like the gazebo idea. And you're right, Betsy, tonight is a special night. Calico just graduated from ASU with a bachelor's in accounting. She's taking the CPA exam in a few days."

Oh, Pierce, don't, Calico thought. She didn't want the spotlight shifted to her. Mr. and Mrs. Brooks were of a social level Pierce was accustomed to, but Calico most definitely was not. If they asked her if she managed her own investment portfolio, she'd die on the spot.

"Accounting?" Betsy said, then laughed. "Calico, you are looking at the woman who nearly single-handedly organized the Starlight Charity Ball last year, which raised a quarter of a million dollars, and was written up in *The Arizona Republic* and *The New York Times.*"

Okay, Calico thought miserably, she got the point. A bachelor's degree in accounting was no big deal.

"Then, guess what?" Betsy went on, smiling. "While I was still all puffed up with my own importance over the success of the ball, the bank called and said I'd overdrawn my personal checking account."

"Again," Jack said, chuckling. "It's hopeless. Betsy and a checking account are a disaster waiting to happen."

"It's true," Betsy said. "And here you sit with a degree in accounting. That is beyond my scope of feasibility. I'm in awe, I really am. My sincerest congratulations, dear."

"Thank you," Calico said, a genuine smile

forming on her lips. "I enjoy math, working with numbers, and the mysteries of income tax forms. It's very challenging."

"Ugh," Betsy said. "The mere thought of all that gives me cold chills. I really do admire you more than I can say, but I'll stick with my committees. Pierce, you have a prize here. Calico is lovely *and* intelligent."

"Believe me, I'm aware of that," Pierce said.

"Come along, Jack," Betsy said. "Let's leave these two in peace."

"Here's my business card, Calico," Jack said. "I don't know what the needs of our accounting department are in regard to personnel. I do, however, insist that everyone on our staff be a CPA. When you pass that exam, drop by and I'll check into the situation if you're at all interested."

"Thank you so much," Calico said. "I really do appreciate this."

"My pleasure," Jack said. "Next week, Pierce. I'm determined to have a gazebo."

Good-byes were said all around, then Jack and Betsy walked away, waving to people across the room as they went. Calico sank back in her chair and stared at the card in her hand.

"I don't believe this," she said.

"Why?" Pierce asked. "Because Jack Brooks is probably worth three or four million dollars and you actually had a conversation with him? Because Jack and Betsy are of a different social status than you, yet Betsy complimented you? Don't you see, Calico? It doesn't matter. An excellent accountant is an asset to any corporation. Your personal background doesn't have anything to do with it. Betsy and Jack accepted you for the person you are. They didn't ask to see your bank balance before they agreed to talk to you. Am I getting through to you on this issue at least?"

"Yes," she said slowly. "Yes, I think you really are. I've been a reverse snob." She tucked the business card into her clutch purse. "If I start to do it again, I'll look at that business card to remind me that I have a college degree that is just as good as anyone else's."

"Fantastic," Pierce said, smiling. "We're making progress here. Eat your green beans, Calico. They're very good for you."

Dessert was fresh strawberries in cream, and champagne. Pierce lifted the fluted glass and toasted Calico's degree, the future, and said that he loved her more than words could say. Calico blinked away tears of happiness, and clinked her glass gently against his.

After sipping cups of rich, cinnamon-flavored coffee, they left the dining room and walked across the entryway to a dimly lit ballroom, where a band was playing and people were dancing. The gleaming dance floor was edged by a carpeted area containing easy chairs and small tables.

Cinderella Smith, Calico thought dreamily, was definitely at a fairy-tale ball with her Prince Charming Pierce.

He led her to one of the tables and flipped over

a card held in a tiny crystal stand to show the word 'occupied.' After ordering mineral water with a twist of lemon and a soft drink from a passing waitress, he turned to Calico.

"May I have this dance, ma'am?"

"I'd be delighted, sir."

Moments later she was swept into his arms, and they were dancing to the dreamy music of a waltz.

Delighted was not quite the word, Calico thought. Heavenly was much better, because to be there in Pierce's arms was, indeed, heaven itself. He felt so good, and smelled so good, and within his embrace, she was cherished and protected.

This was his world, she mused, and tonight she was a part of it. She had a business card in her purse that proved her degree, her talents, were respected. Her dress was as lovely as any other in that room. She and Pierce danced together with ease and grace, as though they'd been doing it for years.

But still, she knew, the obstacle of her monetary debt stood between them, refusing to budge out of the path that would lead her to eternal bliss with Pierce.

Not tonight, Calico, she admonished herself. She was not going to think about that tonight. These were stolen, wondrous hours that belonged to her and Pierce.

When the band took a break, Calico and Pierce finally returned to the small table and sipped their neglected drinks, which were rather watery from melted ice cubes.

"It's warm in here," Pierce said. "Let's go out onto the terrace for a bit, all right? There's a nice garden beyond it."

"That sounds lovely," Calico said, "but what about your allergies? Where there's a garden, there are usually flowers."

He looked at her for a long moment. "I love you, Calico," he said finally. "I can't remember when anyone took my allergies seriously. I've always gotten the feeling that . . . Well, that people sort of snickered at my ailments, my concerns about proper diet, clean air, and all that."

"I realize it's all very important to you, Pierce. Perhaps," she added diplomatically, "you overdo in some areas, but I respect your right to place a great deal of emphasis on the things that you do." She smiled. "And I hereby confess that I don't really believe oat bran muffins are gross."

He laughed and brushed his lips over hers, then stood, extending one hand to her.

"Let's go outside."

The terrace reminded Calico of one that might be part of a plantation home in the South. It was wide and long, with a railing and steps that led down to a garden dotted with gaslights mounted on black posts. The terrace had white wrought iron benches with intricate lattice work. Matching benches were placed along the path through the garden.

Standing at the railing, Calico took a deep

breath and let it out slowly. "Nature's perfume. The flowers smell so good. Don't breathe, Pierce."

He chuckled. "I took an allergy pill before I left home. And don't worry—these pills don't cause drowsiness. Besides, a sneezing attack wouldn't dare intrude on this night. It's too special. It's ours."

"You're a romantic, Pierce Anderson."

He nodded. "I guess I am, which is fine with me. I'm also in love, which is also fine with me." He reached into his jacket pocket and withdrew a small blue velvet box. When he snapped it open a heart-shaped diamond ring in a gold setting sparkled in the starlight. "Calico, this is for you, if you'll accept it."

She stared at the ring, feeling an icy fist clutch her heart.

"Oh, Pierce, it's beautiful, it's . . ." She met his gaze. "I can't take it. You know that. I admit that there isn't as much standing in our way as I once thought. I've grown up, and I've come to realize that I had some immature notions that I apparently formed when I was a child. But that still doesn't erase the fact that I'm not free. I *must* pay off my loans. It's so much money . . . thousands of dollars. I have to do it on my own to be true to myself, to who I am."

"Just listen a minute. Please? You've changed your views on social status, or whatever you want to call it. I'm clinging to the hope that you'll see the light about the money you owe too."

"No, I won't, because—"

"Let me finish. I'm not accepting defeat. We've come so far, and there's only this one issue left that's standing in our way. We'll find the answer, Calico, if we're determined to. Together we can do anything."

"There are some things that just can't be changed, Pierce. No one will wave a magic wand and make my monetary obligations disappear. I can't ask you to wait for heaven only knows how long until I pay them off, and I can't accept your help. Oh, Pierce, it's all so hopeless."

"No, dammit, it isn't. We just haven't found the right solution yet, that's all. Calico, let's compromise about this ring. We'll be engaged to be engaged."

"I beg your pardon?"

"Instead of your wearing it as an engagement ring, I'll put it on your right hand. When we find the answer to this one last problem, we'll put it on your left hand, and it will be official. For now, we're engaged to be engaged."

"I've never heard of such a thing."

He shrugged. "I made it up. What difference does it make? It's a workable solution for us for the time being. Will you do it?"

"Well . . . Oh, dear, you boggle my brain."

"Say 'yes.' It's as simple as that. There's nothing boggling about it. Calico, say 'yes.'"

"Yes," she whispered.

"Thank you." He took the ring from the box and lifted her right hand. "I love you, Calico Smith, and with this ring I'm telling the world that I do. As of this moment, we're engaged to be engaged." He slipped the ring into place.

Calico stared at it for a long moment, until she could barely see it due to the tears misting her eyes. Then she looked at Pierce.

"I love you so much," she said, a sob catching in her throat. "I wish . . ."

"We'll find that answer." He drew her into his arms. "I swear we will."

Their lips met, and her arms twined around his neck. Leaning into him, she molded her body to his, wanting him, aching for the ecstasy that she knew their lovemaking would bring. Her heart suddenly seemed to be singing Pierce's name, over and over.

Oh, Lord, Pierce thought, he had to end this kiss soon. His control had been pushed to the brink already from dancing so many slow songs with Calico nestled against him.

Calico . . . Step by step, he was making her his. The ring on her right hand could be shifted to the left one, then a wedding band added. They'd already removed so many of the obstacles in their path. If only he could discover the solution to paying off her student loans. She wasn't giving an inch. It was *her* goal, and she was determined not to share the burden. Damn, there had to be an answer.

But right now, he knew, this kiss had to end.

He lifted his mouth from hers and drew a ragged breath.

"Calico, I have to stop kissing you," he said

roughly, "or we'll be arrested for what would take place on this terrace."

She blinked, then nodded.

"Yes, you're right. I forgot where we were." She reluctantly loosened her hold on his neck, and stepped back, slowly sliding her hands down his chest. The heart-shaped diamond glittered in the starlight. "It's just so lovely," she said, looking at the ring.

But it was on the wrong hand! Pierce nearly yelled. Patience, Anderson, he told himself. He was still in desperate need of a hefty dose of patience.

"Would you like to dance again?" he asked. "Or have a fresh drink? Or another dessert?"

She gazed into his dark eyes. "No," she said softly. "I'd like to go to your apartment now, Pierce. I'd like to close the door on the world and be alone with you."

"That," he said, slipping one arm across her shoulders, "can be arranged."

As they drove away from the restaurant, neither spoke. The sensuality between them seemed to crackle through the air. They were acutely aware of each other, every movement, every breath taken, heightening their passions even more.

In Pierce's apartment, the single lamp he'd left on cast a muted glow over the large living room. He closed the door, flipped the lock into place, then spun around, trapping Calico between the door and his body.

She leaned against the door and met his smoldering gaze. Heat throbbed through her body, welcomed heat, the heat of desire.

This magic night, she thought dreamily, was far from over. She would offer her body to this magnificent man, the man she loved, and they would soar to the heavens to dance among the silvery stars that had beckoned to them from the summer sky.

Tomorrow would be soon enough to return to reality and the undeniable truth. Tonight there was only Pierce.

He inched closer, his body just barely touching hers, then lowered his head. He kissed each of her cheeks, the tip of her nose, then brushed his lips over hers, teasing her, tantalizing her, causing her to shiver with anticipation of what was to come.

His fingers wove through her silky curls, then his mouth captured hers, his tongue parting her lips to delve deeply within the sweetness beyond in a searing kiss that stole the breath from her body. Her tongue met his to stroke, duel, and a groan rumbled in his chest.

He broke the kiss, and without speaking, they crossed the room and entered his bedroom. He snapped on a lamp, and they shed their clothes quickly, urgently, burning with want and need.

They tumbled onto the bed, their mouths locked together, their hands never still as they touched, caressed, savored. Pierce shifted lower to flick his tongue over her breasts, first one, then the other, bringing the nipples to taut buttons. Then he drew one breast into his mouth and suckled in a rhythm that matched the ache thrumming low within her.

"Oh, Pierce," she said, with a near sob. "Please, Pierce, now. Come to me now."

He sought her mouth once more, then moved over her.

"I love you, Calico," he said, his voice hoarse with passion.

And then he entered her with one deep thrust, filling her deeply, so deeply, until it was impossible to discern his body from hers. They were one. Complete. Joined in glorious ecstasy, they waited a heart-stopping moment to savor the wondrous union before beginning the rocking tempo.

Pierce thundered within Calico's moist haven, and she matched him beat by pounding beat. Wrapping her legs around him, she urged him on, lifting her hips to meet him.

Tension gathered within her in a hot, swirling spiral that centered low, tightening. She clung to Pierce's shoulders as she felt herself soar upward, reaching, nearing the summit that she sought.

"Pierce!"

"Yes!"

They exploded amidst the sparkling stars, holding fast, as they were hurled beyond rapture.

They hovered there, suspended in time in

their wondrous place, then slowly floated back to reality. Pierce collapsed against her, then with his last ounce of energy, rolled onto his back, taking her with him. She buried her face in the crook of his neck as tears of joy misted her eyes.

"Oh, Pierce," she whispered, "that was so beautiful, so exquisitely beautiful."

"Yes," he said, tightening his hold on her. "Yes, it was." He took a deep, steadying breath. "Incredible. Think about it, Calico. For the rest of our lives, we'll be together. Through the good days and bad, and all the lovemaking nights like this one, we'll be together." He paused. "Calico? Are you listening?"

"I—I don't want to think beyond this moment, Pierce," she said softly. "This is a night of magic, not quite real, a Cinderella night."

"Not real? Yes, it is. That's part of what's so wonderful about it all. It's ours. All we have to do is reach out and take it. What's forever for, Calico, if not to make plans, share dreams, of what we'll have?"

"Oh, Pierce, don't, please. Let's not talk anymore now. All right? I feel so heavenly, and sleepy." She wiggled off of him and nestled close to his side. "Mmm. No serious discussions, not tonight."

"Okay," he said quietly.

Damn, he thought, he'd said too much. He'd forgotten his own vow of patience and gone on about the future. He shouldn't have done that, but his question was valid. What was forever for, if not to belong to two people in love?

How long was he going to have to wait until he was allowed to live past the moment at hand?

How much patience was one man expected to have?

When would Calico really be his?

Ten

"Yoo-hoo, Calico?" Abby called, knocking on the door. "May I enter your hovel?"

"You're granted a five-minute audience," Calico hollered. "Come in and talk fast."

Abby strode into the room, straight to the bed, where Calico sat surrounded by papers and books.

"This is nutso," Abby said, planting her hands on her hips. "You've been in here with your nose buried in that junk since Saturday afternoon. I assume you've emerged to eat and shower. This is supper hour on Tuesday, kid. Enough is enough. You probably know that stuff better than the megabrains giving the CPA exam."

"Abby, I have to be certain I've reviewed everything. The test is eight hours a day for three days, starting tomorrow." Her hands flew to her cheeks. "Oh, Lord, the test starts tomorrow."

"Calm down. You're going to ace it. How does

Pierce feel about not having been allowed to see you or speak to you since he brought you back here on Saturday?"

"He's not thrilled, but he's got to understand that this test has top priority right now."

"And after the test, getting a job is top priority, then comes paying off your student loans. For crying out loud, Calico, how long do you expect Pierce Anderson to stand around amusing himself by eating oat bran? He loves you, you love him, and you're running the risk of losing him because of your stubbornness, your misplaced independence, your refusal to compromise. This whole situation is ridiculous . . . and sad. There. I've had my say. Close your mouth. You look like Homer."

Calico snapped her mouth closed, but her gaze remained fixed on Abby.

"And another thing," Abby suddenly said. "I accepted a job today with a fresh-out-of-law-school attorney. He wants to have his own practice from day one. He also wants to have everything done on a computer for the highest efficiency. That's where I come in."

"Congratulations on—"

"Quiet. I was also offered a position with an advertising firm in downtown Phoenix at twice—pay attention, Calico—twice the money, plus full benefits. I turned it down."

"Why? Abby, you have a student loan to pay off too. It's not as much as mine, but it's there. Twice the money? Are you crazy?"

"No, I'm in love with Sticks Statler. The advertising firm said they often work far into the night brainstorming on ad campaigns. I'd do the graphics on a computer, be part of, quote, the team. They give hefty bonuses when they land a big account. They live, breathe, eat, sleep advertising. The attorney I'll be working for said he'll have set office hours because he has a wife he wants to get home to."

"But—"

"Calico, I'll pay off my student loan. It means that I'll have to live in this house for another year instead of getting my own apartment, but that's fine. I'll have a nice balance in my life. Sticks, a job I'm certain I'm going to like, and time for me."

"Abby, you have a folder that's inches thick with pictures from magazines with ideas on how to decorate. You've been planning on that apartment for over a year, ever since the first picture went into that file. I don't believe this."

"Calico, an apartment is a—a materialistic thing. Sticks is the man I love. This wasn't a difficult decision for me to make. I compromised, and now I'll have the best of all of it. So what if I live here another year? What good is a fancy apartment if I'm too busy to enjoy it? What's the point in making double the money if it means I could lose Sticks because I simply wouldn't have enough time to spend with him?"

"Abby, do you realize what you're doing?"

"Do *you* know what *you're* doing, Calico? You've transformed your financial obligation into a nearly tangible entity. It's like a materialistic object in reverse. Instead of being determined to possess it like I might want a nice apartment, or someone else going for a flashy car, you won't rest until your goal is totally *removed*. Same premise, though. It's the same stinky premise."

Calico narrowed her eyes. "Thanks a lot, Abby," she said tightly. "I happen to believe my personal integrity is important."

"Fine. Snuggle up to your integrity at night. I'm not deciding to live in this place another year because I have a fetish for waiting in line to use the bathroom. It's my way of bending, of showing Sticks how deeply I love him. I'm half of a whole now, Calico, and so are you. The thing is, when the dust settles, you're liable to find that your other half is long gone. You're my best friend, and it breaks my heart to stand by and watch what you're doing. Oh, dammit, I'm going to cry. Good-bye." She left the room, slamming the door behind her.

"No," Calico whispered. "You're wrong. You're totally off base, Abby Kolb." Sudden and unexpected tears filled her eyes and slid down her cheeks. "You're wrong."

She pressed trembling fingers to her lips as her gaze swept over the papers and books spread out on the bed. Standing, she began to pace back and forth, her hands wrapped around her elbows in a protective manner.

Abby was wrong, she repeated to herself. Wanting a—a giant-screen television, or a state-of-the-art stereo system, or whatever, making that desire top priority over committing oneself to a relationship was materialistically shallow and selfish.

To compare that scenario with what she had yet to accomplish before agreeing to marry Pierce was absurd, insane. It was apples and oranges, not even remotely related.

Abby was wrong, she told herself again, a sob catching in her throat. Wasn't she? Yes, of course she was. Abby's theory was totally off the mark. Wasn't it? Oh, dear heaven, she couldn't even think straight any longer.

Pierce, she thought suddenly. She had to see Pierce, had to reaffirm by being with him, if only for a few minutes, that her goal, her priorities were exactly the way they should be. Yes, she had to see Pierce.

Pierce slouched lower in the leather chair and idly pressed a button on the television remote control device. The channels changed one after the next, creating a disconnected, nonsensical series of pictures.

"Forget it," he muttered, and shut off the set.

He put the remote control on the end table, then drummed the fingers of one hand on the arm of the chair.

As had been happening for days, Calico's image filled his mind. He loved her. And inch by agonizingly painful inch, he was losing her. He was miserable, lonely, and mad as hell.

He could not deny any longer that his anger

had heated to the boiling point. Calico had stuffed him on a shelf like a used toy, patted him on the head, and told him to stay put until she had time for him again. She didn't want a husband, she wanted a marionette she could jerk around to do her bidding whenever she could fit him into her schedule. Hell.

He leaned forward and rested his elbows on his knees, staring across the room at nothing.

He hadn't slept well since taking Calico back to her boardinghouse Saturday afternoon. The nights had been filled with hours of tossing and turning, and frustrating questions that had no answers.

Miriam had threatened to shoot him on sight if he didn't stop being so crabby but, dammit, he was suffering from extreme stress. Probably fifteen stress-related diseases were gathering force within him at that very moment.

He lunged to his feet and paced across the living room, thrusting a hand through his hair.

What could he have said or done differently? he asked himself for the umpteenth time. What would have gotten through to Calico and made her realize that her stand on paying off her student loans was going to destroy everything they had? Hell, he didn't know what more he could have done, or might do in the future, to get her to change her stubborn mind.

He was rapidly coming to the conclusion that the situation was hopeless, and that realization increased the intensity of all those miserable, lonely, and mad-as-hell emotions.

A knock sounded at his door, jarring him from his troubled thoughts. He strode across the room and yanked open the door.

"Hello, Pierce," Calico said.

"Calico?" he said, staring at her in confusion.

"Well . . . um . . . Yes, it's me. I know you weren't expecting me, and I should have called first, but . . . Pierce, I need to talk to you if you're not busy. May I come in?"

"Oh. Oh, yes, of course." He stepped back to allow her to enter, then closed the door behind her. When he turned, he saw that she'd crossed the room and was looking at him, her huge tote bag clutched to her breasts. "Would you care to sit down?" he asked.

"No, thank you."

He moved to the leather chair and sank into it, his gaze riveted on her. One minute ticked slowly by, then two. Silence hung in the air like a heavy, dark cloud.

"You said you wanted to talk to me," Pierce finally said. Easy, Anderson, he told himself. He knew his anger was churning close to the surface, threatening to erupt like Mount St. Helens. He had to take it slow and easy. "I'm listening."

"Yes, well, so you are." She cleared her throat. "Pierce, you once said that I was clinging to my monetary obligations just as I hold fast to this tote bag, because I need the security of the familiar."

He nodded. "I felt it was a valid theory."

Couldn't he smile at her just a little? Calico wondered. No, there wasn't a smile within a hundred-mile radius of his face.

"And?" he asked.

"Abby came to my room a while ago and dumped *her* theory on me. She said my debts were, in my mind, something tangible. Paying them off was an obsession, like someone who insists he has to have a spiffy car before he'll commit himself to a relationship."

"Interesting."

"I just . . . I just suddenly felt crushed by doubts and confusion, Pierce. I needed to see you to reaffirm that I'm right in what I'm doing and the way I'm doing it. I had to look at you and say to myself, 'Yes, that's Pierce, the man I love, and I mustn't weaken in my resolve to achieve my goals, because then I wouldn't be me, Calico Smith, and Pierce Anderson fell in love with Calico Smith, and—'"

"Hold it just a damn minute," Pierce interrupted, pushing himself to his feet. "You came all the way across town on a bus, inhaling toxic exhaust fumes, just so that you could recharge your battery and enable yourself to stand firm on your idiotic, misplaced principles?"

"You don't have to yell," Calico said, matching his glare.

"Oh, yes, I do have to yell. You've used up my entire life's supply of patience, Calico, you really have. You're calling all the shots, pushing all the buttons, dictating how high you want me to jump. Well, I've had it. Are you getting this? *I . . . have . . . had . . . enough!* I love you, in sickness and in health, for richer, for poorer. Zero in on that one, Calico. For richer, for poorer."

"Pierce—"

"No," he said, slicing one hand through the air. "I honestly believe that what I said about your hanging on to your debts like a security blanket is true, and what Abby said reinforces that theory. Why can't you see what is so clear to everyone around you? Dammit, Calico, you're throwing us away over a few thousand dollars. That doesn't say much for what we have together."

"What about me?" she asked, her voice rising. "What about my integrity, my self-worth, my pride, my—"

"Listen to yourself," he hollered. "My, my, my. In the singular. You. Just you. That's all you think about. I said *together,* but that might as well be a foreign word to you. *Together* we have a debt that could be taken care of by me writing a check." He snapped his fingers. "That fast."

"No!"

He opened his mouth to reply, but then closed it. His shoulders slumped, and he shook his head.

"Then there's . . ." He stopped speaking and swallowed heavily. ". . . there's nothing more to be said. I love you, Calico, but I can't wait years for you to pay back that money. I wish you would have listened to the grapefruit at The Blue Banana, heard the message that materialistic things—money included—aren't important. I wish . . ." He shook his head again.

Calico felt the ache of tears in her throat as she heard the weary defeat in Pierce's voice, saw the pain in his dark eyes.

She wanted to run to him, fling herself into

his arms, declare her love, and agree to marry him at the earliest possible moment. She wanted to tell him what he so desperately needed to hear: that she would accept his financial help to pay her debts. She wanted Pierce Anderson until she drew her last breath.

But none of those things were going to happen. Neither Pierce nor Abby understood. She had to be true to herself, had to achieve the goals she'd set so long ago, before she could move forward toward new ones.

She realized Pierce couldn't wait that long, but understanding that didn't ease the pain of her heartache, nor stop the tears she could feel tracking down her cheeks.

On trembling legs, she slowly crossed the room, pulling the beautiful heart-shaped ring from her finger as she went. She set it on an end table, then continued to the door.

"Good-bye, Pierce," she whispered. "I'm sorry. I'm so very, very sorry."

He didn't speak, knowing words could never get past the lump in his throat. The door closed behind her, and the soft click reverberated in his head like a gunshot.

His gaze fell on the glittering ring and, with his hand shaking, he lifted it from the table. He went into the bedroom, sat down on the edge of the bed, and opened the drawer to the nightstand.

With infinite care, he set the ring on the yellow feather that had fallen from Calico's chicken suit.

Then Pierce Anderson covered his face with his hands and wept.

Eleven

Calico sat beneath a tree and gazed out over the small, pretty lake at Encanto Park. A smile touched her lips as she recalled the canoe ride there with Pierce, and his rock-the-boat bout of sneezing.

What a glorious day that had been, she mused. It was one of the precious memories tucked away in her heart among so many other treasured moments with Pierce. And they all seemed like a lifetime ago.

Her smile faded, and Calico sighed as she absently watched a family of ducks paddle by.

It had been foolish to come here, she decided. Why torture herself by revisiting a place she'd shared with Pierce? Why relive the days and nights of a past best forgotten? Why, when it had been six weeks and two days since that last, heartbreaking scene in Pierce's apartment?

Because she loved Pierce Anderson, and she would forever.

What was forever for? her heart whispered. What was it for, if not to share dreams and plans, and all her tomorrows with the man she loved? But she had lost Pierce because of her pride, her insecurities, which she'd hung on to like a panicked child.

And because, she mentally added, managing to smile a little, because she hadn't listened to the grapefruit at The Blue Banana.

She leaned back against the tree, pulling her knees up and wrapping her arms around them.

Over the past weeks, she'd come face-to-face with the truth. What both Pierce and Abby had said about her obsession to pay off her debt had been true. She'd clung to the loans as a connection to a time that held no surprises or mysteries, a time when Gran had been alive; when life had been hard work and fatigue, but had possessed a limited, narrow, and safe path to travel.

But then she'd found Pierce. And love.

And fear. Unknowns. Unanswered questions. Exquisite lovemaking. Laughter and sunshine.

A beautiful ring. Kissing under the stars.

Dreams of forever and all that forever was for.

"Oh, Pierce," she said aloud. "I love you. I miss you so much."

She'd made the first payment on her loan earlier that day, then had stood in the crowded bank and burst into tears as she'd stared at the receipt in her hand. It was nothing more than a piece of paper. She'd lost the only man she'd ever loved in exchange for what would eventually become a shoe box full of lifeless pieces of paper.

She'd been so wrong . . . and so frightened. It was too late to make amends, to attempt to erase the pain she'd seen in Pierce's beautiful eyes. It was six weeks and two days too late.

Calico suddenly stiffened. Or was it? she wondered. Her pride be damned, because it had already caused her enough grief. If there was the slimmest hope, the slightest chance, that she could win back the love of Pierce Anderson, then, by gum, she was going for it.

Frightening? Oh, yes.

Risky? Oh, yes.

Perhaps foolish and hopeless? Oh, yes.

Worth it?

"Oh, yes," she said, jumping to her feet. "Because Pierce Anderson is what forever is for!"

Two nights later, Calico sat at one of the small tables at The Blue Banana. Very few people were in the coffeehouse, which was par for midweek, and she had a clear view of the door. She took a sip of her soft drink, then glanced at the entrance again as she heard the door open. Her eyes widened in shock as a couple walked in.

"Oh, good night," she mumbled. "I really don't believe this."

Abby and Sticks strolled toward her wearing belted beige trench coats, battered fedoras, and mirrored sunglasses. Sticks's coat was obviously too small; the sleeves came to the middle of his forearms and the bottom hem stopped well above his knees. They slid onto the chairs at Calico's table.

"I have never," Calico said, unable to keep a straight face, "seen you two before in my life."

"Excellent, sweetheart," Sticks said out of the corner of his mouth. "That means our disguises are first-rate."

She laughed. "They're ridiculous. And you do a lousy Bogart, Sticks."

He shrugged. "You can't expect perfection from free labor."

Calico's smile disappeared. "I know, and I can't thank you both enough for—"

"Yoo-hoo, Calico," Abby said, holding up one hand. "We don't need another thank-you speech. Honest. We're glad to help. You finally came out of your stupid stupor and you're leaping into action."

"My stupid stupor?"

"What would *you* call it?"

Calico sighed. "You're right. I was so—"

"Okay, okay," Sticks said, before Calico could launch into another "How could I have been so blind?" speech. "Let's compare notes and give our reports."

"Check," Abby said.

"Would you mind taking off the sunglasses?" Calico asked. "It's rather disconcerting to be talking to so many images of myself."

"Well, darn," Abby said, doing as instructed, "these are terrific shades. Okay. Sticks and I slinked into—"

"Sticks slinked?"

"Like a pro," he said, appearing very pleased with himself.

"May I have the floor here?" Abby asked.

"Sorry," Calico said. "Carry on."

"Thank you. Now then, Sticks and I watched Pierce's office building—roasting our bodies in the heat, mind you—until he went to lunch. Then we slinked into his office and chatted with Miriam, his secretary. You'd like her, Calico. She's spunky like Gran was."

"Yeah," Sticks said. "Miriam is a cool lady."

"Anyway," Abby went on, "Miriam said that Pierce has been very down, quiet, no zip-a-dee-do-da at all since you two broke it off. She'd swear on his mother's bridge cards—that's a direct quote—that he is *not* seeing another woman. He's a slug. Works, goes home, works, goes home. Miriam said she's keeping her fingers crossed for you. So, that coast is clear. Pierce has not replaced you in any way, shape, or form."

"Check," Sticks said. "We also saw my buddy Franko, and we're all set with what you need. Hoop says the car is gassed up and ready to go."

"Okay," Calico said. "I spoke with Mrs. Weatherby. There's no problem with getting into Pierce's apartment. They exchanged keys last year as a safety precaution for emergencies. She was so excited. She said this was more romantic than her seasick cruise. Oh, she got Homer a girlfriend named Harriet. Anyway, I have the key to Pierce's apartment." She paused. "I also have an army of butterflies in my stomach. Oh, Lord, I can't do this. Cancel that. I can and I will."

"Check," Abby said. Calico suddenly gazed at her friends in distress. "But what if Pierce tells me to take a hike? What if he fell *out* of love with me during these weeks? What if—"

"—you put a cork in it?" Sticks interrupted. "All systems are go. Tomorrow is Operation Ambush Anderson."

"Tomorrow, we hope," Abby said quietly, "is the first day of Calico and Pierce's forever."

The next evening, Pierce stepped out of the elevator on his floor and stopped. The elevator doors swished closed as he stood staring down the silent corridor.

He did not want to spend another long, dreary night within his empty apartment. Yet not one mental suggestion he'd offered himself as an alternative held an ounce of appeal.

Ah, hell, he thought, he was a wreck. He missed Calico more with every interminable day and restless night. He loved her so damn much. He needed her, wanted her, ached for her. The rest of his life stretched before him like an endless and lonely road.

"I want my chicken back, dammit," he said aloud.

He sighed, admitted yet again that he did not have a magical solution that would bring Calico back to him, and walked slowly down the hall to his apartment. He unlocked the door, stepped inside, and closed the door behind him.

Then he stiffened so suddenly, his muscles protested at the tension. His mouth dropped open, his eyes widened, and in shock and disbelief, he swept his gaze over his living room.

Grapefruit.

Every inch of the entire floor was covered with round, yellow grapefruit.

There were big grapefruit, small grapefruit, varying shades of grapefruit, but there was no denying the astonishing fact that those things were most definitely grapefruit.

"What . . . Who . . . Why . . ." he babbled. He pressed one hand to his forehead. "No temperature. Oh, dear Lord, that means I've totally lost it. I've had my nervous breakdown. It's here in the form of a grapefruit. I'm bonkers."

"No, you're not," a soft voice said. "You're not crazy. You're very loved."

He snatched his hand from his head and spun around to see Calico standing by the kitchen. She walked into the living room, carefully nudging grapefruit from her path as she came. She stopped in the middle of the room.

"Calico?" he said.

His gaze flickered over her, dressed in a pretty, flowered wraparound skirt and a pale blue blouse, and the tempo of his heart increased tenfold.

She was exquisite, he thought, and he loved her so much. But what was she doing there, and why had his apartment been redecorated with grapefruit?

"Pierce," Calico said, wishing her voice was steadier, "I've missed you so very much. I love you more than I can ever begin to tell you, and I'm asking you to forgive me for being so wrong and refusing to listen to you."

"I love you, too, Calico," he said, "but it's rather difficult to digest what you're saying when there are a couple hundred grapefruit staring at me. Could we cover that first? I mean, have you taken up selling grapefruit door-to-door? Speaking of doors, how did you get through mine? Forget that. Concentrate on the grapefruit."

"It's my statement," she said. "It's tangible, positive proof that I've changed my outlook. Remember the grapefruit from The Blue Banana? The message was that material things don't matter. My student loans had become, in my mind, material objects. These"—she swept one arm through the air—"are my way of telling you that I realize how wrong I was, and how right you were. I had my priorities all scrambled up, and I allowed my pride too much space, and . . . Oh, Pierce, I'm so sorry."

He nodded. "The 'Ode to a Grapefruit.' Yes, of course, I remember." He scrutinized the floor again. "When you make a statement, you don't mess around." He ran one hand over the back of his neck. "Calico, my life has been hell since you left. It's empty, drab, and I'm so damn lonely. I'm listening to what you're telling me, but . . ." He shook his head.

"But?" she whispered, a shiver coursing through her.

"But it's the timing of all of this. You refused my help, put me, us, on hold until you passed your CPA exam and got a job. You also said the debt had to be paid off, too, before we could be together. So, okay, you've given in some on that part, but I imagine you've started making payments on the loans."

"Yes, I have, but—"

"Dammit. I want this to feel right, Calico, to end this hell, but it doesn't. You're still dictating the terms. *Now,* you're saying, we can be together, because you've got a handle on everything else. That's not sharing, living vows of 'for richer, for poorer.' Why didn't you trust in our forever enough to come to me with your debts in tow? Sure, you still owe money, but you made certain you have a means to pay it off. You stuck me in a corner while you did it all exactly the way you wanted to, with a small amount of compromise that's supposed to satisfy me. No, Calico, this just doesn't feel right at all."

Hope began to grow within her, but she ruthlessly tamped it down. She had to be sure. "You're telling me that you'd really believe I've changed if I hadn't already passed the CPA exam? You're hurt and wary of my kind of love, my depth of commitment, because I refused to make myself vulnerable by asking for your help with the debt?"

"Yes, that's pretty much it, I guess. You can't turn love on and off, Calico, to suit your purposes. We're supposed to share the good, the bad, and everything in between. The way you handled this scares the hell out of me. What else will you decide to do on your own? Where's my voice in this relationship? Oh, damn, I wish you'd have listened to the grapefruit sooner."

Calico smiled. The smile grew, lighting up her face, sparkling in her eyes.

"Pierce Anderson, I love you," she said. "I want to marry you, have your babies, grow old with you. Pierce, I did take the CPA exam."

"I know," he said. "I know."

"But, my darling Pierce, they won't notify me for three months from the exam date about the results."

He gaped at her. "What?"

"I'm working at a fast-food restaurant while I'm waiting to hear. I've managed to make one payment on my loan only because I get to eat hamburgers for free for as long as I can stand them."

"Calico, are you saying? . . ."

"Oh, yes, Pierce. I'm coming to you just as I am, for richer, for poorer, until death parts us. Pierce, please, please, forgive me for my mistakes. Let's start fresh from right now, this very moment. You and I, together, we are what forever is for."

Pierce took a deep breath and let it out slowly. He stared up at the ceiling for a long moment, striving to retain control of emotions that were slipping from his command. He lost the battle, and when he met Calico's gaze again, tears glistened in his eyes, matching the tears misting hers.

He held out one hand to her. "Come here," he said, his voice husky. "Please, Calico. I need you, I love you. Marry me."

"Oh, Pierce."

She shuffled toward him as quickly as she could move the grapefruit out of her way. Then at last, *at last,* she flung herself into his embrace, wrapping her arms around his neck. Their lips met in a deep, searing kiss, and the despair and loneliness of the past weeks were forgotten.

Calico Smith and Pierce Anderson began their journey toward forever.

The wedding present they received from Abby and Sticks was given a place of honor in the bride and groom's new home. It was a custom-ordered painting of a grapefruit and a bright yellow feather.

THE EDITOR'S CORNER

What an irresistible line-up of romance reading you have coming your way next month. Truly, you're going to be **LOVESWEPT** by these stories that are guaranteed to heat your blood and keep you warm throughout the cold, winter days ahead.

First on the list is **WINTER BRIDE**, LOVESWEPT #522, by the ever-popular Iris Johansen. Ysabel Belfort would trade Jed Corbin anything for his help on a perilous mission—her return to her South American island home, to recover what she'd been forced to leave behind. But he demands her sensual surrender, arousing her with a fierce pleasure, until they're engulfed in a whirlwind of danger and desire. . . . A gripping and passionate love story, from one of the genre's premier authors.

You'll be **BEWITCHED** by Victoria Leigh's newest LOVESWEPT, #523, as Hank Alton is when he meets Sally. According to his son, who tried to steal her apples, she's a horribly ugly witch, but instead Hank discovers a reclusive enchantress whose eyes shimmer with warmth and mystery. A tragedy had sent Sally Michaels in search of privacy, but Hank shatters her loneliness with tender caresses and burning kisses. Victoria gives us a shining example of the power of love in this touching romance guaranteed to bring a smile to your face and tears to your eyes.

Judy Gill creates a **GOLDEN WARRIOR**, LOVESWEPT #524, in Eric Lind, for he's utterly masculine, outrageously sexy, and has a rake's reputation to match! But Sylvia Mathieson knows better than to get lost in his bluer-than-blue eyes. He claims to need the soothing fire of her love, and she aches to feel the heat of his body against hers, but could a pilot who roams the skies ever choose to make his home in her arms? The sensual battles these two engage in will keep you turning the pages of this fabulous story from Judy.

Please give a big welcome to brand-new author Diane Pershing and her first book, **SULTRY WHISPERS**, LOVESWEPT #525. Lucas Barabee makes Hannah Green melt as he woos her with hot lips and steamy embraces. But although she wants the job he offered, she knows only too well the danger of mixing business with pleasure. You'll delight in the sweet talk and irresistible moves Lucas must use to convince Hannah she can trust him with her heart. A wonderful romance by one of our New Faces of '92!

In **ISLAND LOVER**, LOVESWEPT #526, Patt Bucheister sweeps you away to romantic Hawaii, where hard-driving executive Judd Stafford has been forced to take a vacation. Still, nothing can distract him . . . until he meets Erin Callahan. Holding her is like riding a roller coaster of emotions—all ups and downs and stomach-twisting joy. But Erin has fought hard for her independence, and she isn't about to make it easy for Judd to win her over. This love story is a treat, from beginning to end!

Laura Taylor has given her hero quite a dilemma in **PROMISES**, LOVESWEPT #527. Josh Wyatt has traveled to the home he's never known, intending to refuse the inheritance his late grandfather has left him, but executor Megan Montgomery is determined to change his mind. A survivor and a loner all his life, Josh resists her efforts, but he can't ignore the inferno of need she arouses in him, the yearning to experience how it feels to be loved at last. Laura has outdone herself in crafting a story of immense emotional impact.

Look for four spectacular books this month from FAN-FARE. Bestselling author Nora Roberts will once again win your praise with **CARNAL INNOCENCE**, a riveting contemporary novel where Caroline Waverly learns that even in a sleepy town called Innocence, secrets have no place to hide, and in the heat of steamy summer night it takes only a single spark to ignite a deadly crime of passion. Lucy Kidd delivers **A ROSE WITHOUT THORNS**, a compelling historical romance set in eighteenth-century England. Susannah Bry's world is turned upside-down when her father sends her to England to live with wealthy relatives, and she meets the bold and dashing actor Nicholas Carrick. New author Alexandra Thorne will dazzle you with the contemporary novel **DESERT HEAT**. In a world of fiery beauty, lit by a scorching desert sun, three very different women will dare to seize their dreams of glory . . . and irresistible love. And, Suzanne Robinson will captivate you with **LADY GALLANT**, a thrilling historical romance in the bestselling tradition of Amanda Quick and Iris Johansen. A daring spy in Queen Mary's court, Eleanora Becket meets her match in Christian de Rivers, a lusty, sword-wielding rogue, who has his own secrets to keep, his own enemies to rout—and his own brand of vengeance for the wide-eyed beauty whom he loved too well. Four terrific books from FANFARE, where you'll find only the best in women's fiction.

Happy Reading!

With warmest wishes for a new year filled with the best things in life,

Nita Taublib

Nita Taublib
Associate Publisher / LOVESWEPT
Publishing Associate / FANFARE

Don't miss these fabulous
Bantam Fanfare titles
on sale in December.

CARNAL INNOCENCE
by Nora Roberts

A ROSE WITHOUT THORNS
by Lucy Kidd

DESERT HEAT
by Alexandra Thorne

LADY GALLANT
by Suzanne Robinson

Ask for them by name.

CARNAL INNOCENCE

By Nora Roberts
author of
GENUINE LIES
and PUBLIC SECRETS

Even the innocent have secrets to hide . . .

Strangers don't stay strangers for long in Innocence, Mississippi, as witty, urbane, and beautiful Caroline Waverly is quick to discover. Fame has taken its toll on the celebrated concert violinist, what with grueling tours and high-pressure performances, climaxing in an all-too-public break-up with the world-class conductor who is also her lover.

All Caroline wants from her stay in Innocence is a chance to be out of the spotlight—to live quietly in her family's secluded old bayou home with its lace-curtained windows and shady front porch. But what she is about to learn is that even in a town called Innocence secrets have no place to hide, and in the heat of a steamy summer night it only takes a single spark to ignite a deadly crime of passion.

For the sleepy bliss of Innocence is shattered forever by the deadly strikes of a killer at large, and Caroline falls under the spell of a town with a darkly deceptive nature . . . and a smooth-talking, irresistible Southern Charmer named Tucker Longstreet whose seductive touch awakens her own carnal desires—and ensnares her in a killer's crazed dreams.

A ROSE WITHOUT THORNS

By Lucy Kidd

Set in Eighteenth-century England, A ROSE WITHOUT THORNS tells the story of Susannah Bry, a young Virginian whose bankrupt father has sent her to England to her wealthy relatives there. In this scene Susannah has her first encounter with Nicholas Carrick, an actor who will become her lover. . . .

And as the door closed she was the only one inside. She had determined it: she would not follow him, moping after him, just because, by chance, she had once danced with him. *Carrick.* "Damn!" she whispered, scraping wax from the table with her nails; she did not know why. She looked around at the green-walled dining chamber with its smoking sconces; at the rose-colored closet to one side and the row of doors leading to empty rooms on the other. For all their luxury—their gilt furniture, their wall panels painted with cherubs—the rooms had a dusty, neglected air, all the more marked when they were empty.

The others had been outdoors, it seemed, an age. Curiosity overcame her. She stood and walked to the door, and half opened it.

"You don't mean to deny," a mild-voiced man, a

barrister, was saying, "that the institution of marriage has its practical *uses*. . . ."

"Ha!" A big, square-built, red-faced man threw back his head, laughing, and while some of the ladies tittered, the barrister queried, "Would you not agree, Mr. Carrick, with Dr. Johnson's words: that 'Marriage has many pains, but celibacy has no pleasures'?"

At the sound of his name again, *Carrick*, Susannah felt her heart begin to pound. *Why should I care?* she thought. A cold wind grazed her shoulders. *What should I care what he thinks on marriage?* The door beside her creaked, and at the sound Carrick's gaze moved up and found her.

"Why, I'm no enemy of marriage," he said, with a lazy nod at the barrister. Again, almost insolently, he stared up, across the terrace. "Why, a happy marriage must be perfection. A rose without thorns. And"—he began to move through the crowd—"you're just as likely of finding it."

Now he faced Susannah. Quickly, before she was able to speak, he reached up to the bosom of her dress and tugged the rose, on its thin stem, free. Her scarf drifted loose, and he caught it.

She felt the cold air on her skin, yet still could not move as, smiling, he wound the scarf around her wrist and tucked the rose into his buttonhole. Her heart-beats sounded in her ears. As she slid back through the door, she forced a smile to her lips. For a second she watched Carrick and the others; then, as the crowd began to stream in again, she ran for the safety of the empty closet.

She hid in that chamber, with its mirrors and pink walls, trying to pull her dress higher, feeling her face go alternately hot and pale. Outside she had been so tongue-tied and foolish. *Because of him?* She heard the chatter in the other rooms growing louder. She leaned against the window frame, watching her reflection in the mirror opposite. For a moment she felt at peace. Then something moved in the smoky light of the doorway.

She looked over, and her heart began to pound again. Carrick was standing there. She could see only a silhouette: a compact body some inches taller than hers, which he held taught, his arms folded, one foot posed before the other. He seemed to consider her, and slowly walked closer.

If he has come to apologize, Susannah thought, *I will be dignified.* She bit her lip, preparing herself.

But she had no time to remember how. Suddenly Carrick was behind her, his body barely, but decidedly, touching hers. He reached for her hands, then took quick hold of them, sweeping them back behind her. He held them there, his fingers tickling, lightly stroking her palms.

"Where is it you come from?" he said, smiling at their twin reflections in the mirror.

The question surprised her. "Here," she said defensively. "And before that—America."

Her heart beat quickly. Because her dress squeezed her waist in so tightly, all the blood surging through her seemed to rush to what was above and below. Her chest rose and fell quickly with her breathing, and she saw Carrick was looking down at her breasts, at the swell of them. She twisted her hands in his. She knew she ought to escape, for she did not know what she was feeling. The embroidery of his waistcoat grazed the bare skin of her shoulders.

He let go of her hands easily, and smiled. "I did not think they grew such wildflowers in America, as you. I had thought the place inhabited by—drab little Puritans, and savages."

"No. I—" She knew he must expect a witty rebuke.

But she had none. She knew also that she was free to escape now, for he held no part of her. But she did not want to escape. He looked into her eyes—his were black pits, lost to her sight—and, with one hand, then the other, reached below the curling edge of her dress. He lifted her breasts above the cloth, stroking their high curves, and the valley between. The lower half of his body moved against hers. And all the blood that had rushed down there, inside her, was set coursing again as he stroked the tips of her breasts. He did not kiss her. Instead, he tilted his head away, watching her. With a questioning glance, then curiously, deliberately, he stepped back, bending to take the tip of her left breast in his mouth. His tongue worked over it, teasing it, and it felt so good, and yet was such torture, that she had to squirm free. She let out a little cry. He pulled away, then, but returned his hands, teasing her nipples, even pinching them until it seemed to her that there was no feeling in her body but exactly there: there, and in that place between her legs where the flesh was moist and swollen, and finally seemed to have a heartbeat of its own. The blood pulsed and seemed to flow upward, spreading, warming her. She let out a deep breath.

She realized now that her eyes had been closed, and when she opened them she saw Carrick smiling, his teeth glinting in the dark. She let out a low sound of fear, not quite a word, and in answer he kissed her quickly on the forehead. He reached inside his frock coat and pulled out her wrinkled scarf, and as she took it, he plucked the rose, too, from his collar and offered it to her. She shook her head, on a sudden impulse.

He said, "A token?" and smiled back, tucking the rose back into his collar as he left her.

She did not know how long it took for her

breathing to slow, for the color to leave her face. When she had stopped trembling, and righted her scarf and gown, she emerged into the dining chamber, now empty. She knew that her skin was damp, that the paint must be running down her face; but when she saw the others in the next room, she knew they would not notice.

DESERT HEAT

By Alexandra Thorne

A LAND OF FLAMES . . . It is a world of fiery beauty and shadowy dangers, where the arid heat of day ignites the sizzling passions of night . . . and where three very different women pursue their dreams of glory—and irresistible love.

WOMEN OF FIRE . . . Liz, Archer, and Maryann—under an endless sky, lit by sparks, three women ripe with yearning will dare to seize their dreams—but will they be strong enough to keep from getting burned by . . . DESERT HEAT?

In the following excerpt, gallery owner Liz Kant is dining at a restaurant with her lover, Alan, an Apache artist. . . .

She embodied the eternal female mystery—unknowable, unfathomable, and utterly desirable. Tonight she wore a simple black sheath, suspended from her shoulders by narrow straps he had been aching to lower all through dinner.

Liz's coloring made her a painter's dream. She had

flawless ivory skin and shoulder-length, coppery hair framing a face whose perfection still startled him even though ten years had passed since he first saw it. The chiseled planes of her high cheekbones and narrow, slightly aquiline nose offered a fascinating contrast to full, sensual lips that blushed coral without the benefit of makeup. Her eyes were her finest feature. Set beneath well-arched brows and fringed with jet-black lashes, her eyes were the same astonishing shade of blue as Bisbee turquoise.

"I want to make love to you," he blurted out.

"Here?" Mischief sparked in her eyes. "What am I? Dessert?"

"I'll make a fool of myself if we stay here much longer." Reaching for his wallet, he put three fifty-dollar bills on the table. In his haste, he almost knocked his chair over as he got to his feet.

Liz smiled, but her speed matched his as they hurried from the restaurant.

Ten minutes later Alan turned his Blazer onto the steep road that led to Liz's mansion halfway up the flank of Camelback Mountain. He drove automatically, pulled up in front of the house, and walked Liz to the door, while mentally rehearsing what he intended to say later in the evening.

"I want to tell Rosita I'm home, and check for messages," Liz said as he shut the front doors behind them. "How about getting a bottle of champagne and meeting me in the bedroom?"

"Now, that's an offer I can't refuse," he replied. Although he took time to return to his car and retrieve a jeweler's box from the glove compartment, Alan arrived in Liz's bedroom before she did. He set a silver tray bearing a chilled bottle of Perrier-Jouet and two Waterford flutes on the table in front of the fireplace. Then he removed the box from his khaki safari jacket and placed it on the table as well.

Six months before he'd commissioned his friend Ted Charveze, the internationally acclaimed Isleta Pueblo gemologist, to make something special for Liz. Charveze had spent weeks finding exactly the right Bisbee turquoise, flawless stones with depth and zat. "Good diamonds are a hell of a lot easier to come by these days than top-notch turquoise," Charveze had complained, "especially when you insist the stones match Liz's eyes."

The results had been worth waiting for. Charveze, who designed for Cartier, had outdone himself, producing a golden, jewel-inlaid collar that took the form of Avanyu, the sacred life-giving serpent. Now Alan opened the box one last time, adjusting the masterwork in its satin-lined lair. Although money meant little to him personally, he enjoyed being able to give Liz beautiful things. Tonight he wanted to envelop her in his love. The excellent meal and the gift were only a part of the pleasure he planned.

Years ago, when he and Liz became lovers, he quickly realized how little she knew of passion. The first time they went to bed she had faked her orgasm—and not very well at that. Back then, he'd still been a bit in awe of her success, the ease with which she moved through the glitzy world of high-priced art. But that night he pitied her. To be a stranger to her own body, a body so perfectly crafted for sensual delight, seemed a tragedy. It still astonished him that Anglos, despite their cultural preoccupation with sex, could be so untutored in the ways of a man and a woman.

Liz had taught him how to get along in the white world, how to dress, to make small talk, to order in the five-star restaurants she liked to frequent—where being seen at the right table with the right people was more important than filling an empty stomach. In return he brought her, slowly and patiently, to the full realization of her womanhood. Now he was as comfortable dealing with a sommelier as if he'd been to the manner born, and she reveled in the pleasures of the bedroom like the most knowledgeable Apache female. It was, he thought, a fair exchange.

Taking off his jacket, he sat in one of the large armchairs that flanked the fireplace. Liz's bedroom was almost as familiar to him as his own, but he never felt quite at ease in it. His own home was built of adobe and furnished in a rough, masculine fashion, with antiques from Santa Fe, Chimayo rugs, and artifacts from the numerous Indian cultures of the Grand Chimeca. By contrast, Liz's room was ostentatiously, sensually feminine. The walls were mirrored, the floor covered with a thick white Australian wool carpet. The furniture was white too, pickled oak custom-made to Liz's specifications. A quilted, white silk spread covered her oversize fourposter.

The room had been designed as a backdrop for the painting that hung over the fireplace, a four-by-eight-foot portrait of Liz, nude, lying on her bed as if she waited for a lover. As Alan studied the painting, satisfaction warmed his eyes. The portrait, finished six years earlier, had held up well. It was still one of his best works. He'd come very close to doing Liz justice, even though it had been distracting as hell to paint her like that. Grinning, he recalled how much faster he would have completed the canvas if he hadn't stopped so many times to make love to her.

He had wanted Liz from the day he walked into her

gallery. Then, his reaction had been immediate, visceral—desire triumphing over reason. He had never expected to have her, to love and be loved by her. As an impoverished Apache artist, he'd known the Liz Kants of the world were out of his reach.

He'd grown up well schooled in hatred and distrust of whites. His tribal elders had taught that white men had taken everything from the Apaches, their ancestral hunting grounds, their culture, their freedom—even their lives in the bloody, desperate battles of the late 1800s, when government policy had insisted that the only good Indian was a dead Indian. The warrior's death roll—Mangas, Colorado, Victorio, Geronimo, as well as Alan's own ancestors, Cochise and Nachez—was still repeated around countless campfires.

In accordance with his earliest training, Alan had expected to fall in love with a woman of his own people, a girl whose character and fortitude had been tested in the ceremony of the White-Painted Woman, to marry her and have many children as his brothers and sisters had, and to raise them as true Apaches.

Then he'd met Liz, and his expectations had changed irrevocably.

"You look a million miles away," she said, walking into the room and closing the doors behind her. "Is something wrong?"

"I was thinking about us." He paused. This was a momentous evening, and he wanted to do things properly. "I want to talk about our future. But first I have something for you." Taking the case from the table, he placed it in her hands.

Her matchless eyes widened as she opened it. "It's beautiful, Alan," she said throatily, lifting the necklace and clasping it around her neck.

Although he longed to take her in his arms, he poured two glasses of champagne and placed one in her hand. "I've been waiting to talk to you all night. Why don't we sit down."

Liz put her glass down and moved so close to him that her breasts brushed his chest. "I want to thank you properly first."

Enter Loveswept's
Wedding Contest

AH! WEDDINGS! The joyous ritual we cherish in our hearts—the perfect ending to courtship. Brides in exquisite white gowns, flowers cascading from glorious bouquets, handsome men in finely tailored tuxedos, butterflies in stomachs, nervous laughter, music, tears, and smiles. . . . AH! WEDDINGS!! But not all weddings have a predictable storybook ending; sometimes they are much, much more—grooms who faint at the altar, the cherubic ring bearer who drops the band of gold in the lake to see if it will float, traffic jams that strand the bride miles from the church, or the gorgeous hunk of a best man who tempts the bride almost too far. . . . AGHH!! WEDDINGS!!!

LOVESWEPT is celebrating the joy of weddings with a contest for YOU. And true to LOVESWEPT's reputation for innovation, this contest will have THREE WINNERS. Each winner will receive a year of free LOVESWEPTs and the opportunity to discuss the winning story with a LOVESWEPT editor.

Here's the way it goes. We're looking for short wedding stories, real or from your creative imagination, that will fit in one of three categories:

1) THE MOST ROMANTIC WEDDING
2) THE FUNNIEST THING THAT EVER HAPPENED AT A WEDDING
3) THE WEDDING THAT ALMOST WASN'T

This will be LOVESWEPT's first contest in some time for writers and aspiring writers, and we are eagerly anticipating the discovery of some terrific stories. So start thinking about your favorite real-life wedding experiences—or the ones you always wished (or feared?) would happen. Put pen to paper or fingers to keyboard and tell us about those WEDDINGS (AH)!!

For prizes and rules, please see rules, which follow.

BANTAM LOVESWEPT WEDDING CONTEST
OFFICIAL RULES

1. *No purchase necessary.* Enter Bantam's LOVESWEPT WEDDING CONTEST by completing the Official Entry Form below (or handprinting the required information on a plain 3" x 5" card) and writing an original story (5–10 pages in length) about one of the following three subjects: (1) The Most Romantic Wedding, (2) The Funniest Thing That Ever Happened at a Wedding, or (3) The Wedding That Almost Wasn't. Each story must be typed, double spaced, on plain 8 1/2" x 11" paper, and must be headed on the top of the first page with your name, full address, home telephone number, date of birth, and, below that information, the title of the contest subject you selected when you wrote your story. You may enter a story in one, two, or all three contest categories, but a separate Entry Form or Card must accompany each entry, and each entry must be mailed to Bantam in a separate envelope bearing sufficient postage. Completed Entry Forms or Cards, along with your typed story, should be sent to:

   > BANTAM BOOKS
   > LOVESWEPT WEDDING CONTEST
   > Department NT
   > 666 Fifth Avenue
   > New York, New York 10103

   All stories become the property of Bantam Books upon entry, and none will be returned. All stories entered must be original stories that are the sole and exclusive property of the entrant.

2. *First Prizes (3).* Three stories will be selected by the LOVESWEPT editors as winners in the LOVESWEPT WEDDING CONTEST, one story on each subject. The prize to be awarded to the author of the story selected as the First Prize winner of each subject-matter category will be the opportunity to meet with a LOVESWEPT editor to discuss the story idea of the winning entry, as well as publishing opportunities with LOVESWEPT. This meeting will occur at either the Romance Writers of America convention to be held in Chicago in July 1992 or at Bantam's offices in New York City. Any travel and accommodations necessary for the meeting are the responsibility of the contest winners and will not be provided by Bantam, but the winners will be able to select whether they would rather meet in Chicago or New York. If any First Prize winner is unable to travel in order to meet with the editor, that winner will have an opportunity to have the First Prize discussion via an extended telephone conversation with a LOVESWEPT editor. The First Prize winners will also be sent all six LOVESWEPT titles every month for a year (approximate retail value: $200.00).

   Second Prizes (3). One runner-up in each subject-matter category will be sent all six LOVESWEPT titles every month for six months (approximate retail value: $100.00).

3. All completed entries must be postmarked and received by Bantam no later than January 15, 1992. Entrants must be over the age of 21 on the date of entry. Bantam is not responsible for lost or misdirected or incomplete entries. The stories entered in the contest will be judged by Bantam's LOVESWEPT editors, and the winners will be selected on the basis of the originality, creativity, and

writing ability shown in the stories. All of Bantam's decisions are final and binding. Winners will be notified on or about May 1, 1992. Winners have 30 days from date of notice in which to accept their prize award, or an alternative winner will be chosen. If there are insufficient entries or if, in the judges' sole opinion, no entry is suitable or adequately meets any given subject as described above, Bantam reserves the right not to declare a winner for either or both of the prizes in any particular subject-matter category. There will be no prize substitutions allowed and no promise of publication is implied by winning the contest.

4. Each winner will be required to sign an Affidavit of Eligibility and Promotional Release supplied by Bantam. Entering the contest constitutes permission for use of the winner's name, address, biographical data, likeness, and contest story for publicity and promotional purposes, with no additional compensation.

5. The contest is open to residents in the U.S. and Canada, excluding the Province of Quebec, and is void where prohibited by law. All federal and local regulations apply. Employees of Bantam Books, Bantam Doubleday Dell Publishing Group, Inc., their subsidiaries and affiliates, and their immediate family members are ineligible to enter. Taxes, if any, are the responsibility of the winners.

6. For a list of winners, available after June 15, 1992, send a self-addressed stamped envelope to WINNERS LIST, LOVESWEPT WEDDING CONTEST, Department NT, 666 Fifth Avenue, New York, New York 10103.

OFFICIAL ENTRY FORM

BANTAM BOOKS
LOVESWEPT WEDDING CONTEST
Department NT
666 Fifth Avenue
New York, New York 10103

NAME _____

ADDRESS _____

CITY _____ STATE _____ ZIP _____

HOME TELEPHONE NUMBER _____

DATE OF BIRTH _____

CONTEST SUBJECT FOR THIS STORY IS: _____
_____

SIGNATURE CONSENTING TO ENTRY _____
_____